Wild Side of the River

A Western Story

by

MICHAEL ZIMMER

Skyhorse Publishing

www.skyhorsepublishing.com

10 9 8 7 6 5 4 3 2 1

Library of Congress Cataloging-in-Publication Data is available on file.

ISBN: 978-1-62873-640-3

Printed in the United States of America

Wild Side of the River

Chapter One

It wasn't much past midday when Ethan Wilder drew rein on top of the bluff overlooking his family's ranch. Leaning forward with both hands covering the broad horn of his saddle, he studied the ramshackle collection of log and adobe structures closely. Pausing for a few minutes to study the spread from a distance was an old habit of Ethan's, a holdover from when the Sioux used to cross this stretch of northern Montana on their way to and from the Grandmother's land—Canada. The Sioux didn't get up this way much any more, but Ethan still stopped to look every time he came home, whether he'd only been gone a few hours, or, as he had this last time, nearly two months. A pack mule wandered up beside Ethan's bay gelding, long lips nibbling at the autumn-dried buffalo grass. In addition to his personal gear—some cooking utensils, traps, and extra clothing—the mule was carrying nearly two dozen wolf pelts that Ethan intended to turn in to the Montana Cattleman's Association for a bounty, plus a trio of grizzly bear hides he'd taken in the Small Horn Mountains, west of his pa's Bar-Five spread on the Marias River.

The Bar-Five wasn't the biggest spread north of the Marias in that summer of 1884, but it was the oldest. Its roots went back to the American Fur Company trading post Ethan's pa had worked for in the 1850s. What remained of the old post was the family's living quarters now. A small barn and blacksmith shop constructed of logs dragged up from the river, and a corral off the barn's south side, had been added after the fur company abandoned the post in 1865, selling the buildings to Jacob Wilder for a pittance.

Ethan had come to the post as a toddler, but could still remember reaching up to hold onto his mother's hand the first time they'd entered the building. The ex-trading post was the only home Ethan had ever known, or ever wanted to, although its continued existence had been questionable during those early years of the Sioux wars.

Staring down the long slope to the ranch, Ethan's instincts stirred warningly, in a way they hadn't for many a year. Something didn't feel right. It wasn't anything he could see or put a finger on, but it was there, hanging over the broad flat that bordered the feeder creek above the Marias like the smell of rotting meat. Shucking his Winchester, he laid it across his saddlebows, then nudged the bay's ribs with his heels.

Ethan Wilder was a lean, broad-shouldered man of twenty-four, his square jaw heavily stubbled after two months in the wilderness, eyes a blue so pale they sometimes looked gray. He sat his horse with the loose-jointed familiarity of a man who had spent his life in the saddle.

Ethan's pa, Jacob, ran a few head of cattle to pay the bills and keep the family stocked in what couldn't be raised, hunted, or traded for, but ranching had never been his calling. He'd gone into it reluctantly after the buffalo had been shot out, as much to claim the better water holes and springs north of the Marias River than any desire to build a stock-growing empire the way so many others seemed driven to do.

Some of the newer citizens to that part of Montana claimed the only thing Jacob Wilder could raise with any success was hell and sons—he had four of the latter, Ethan being the oldest. Not that Jacob ever gave a damn what others said. His reputation for raising hell was something he cherished, having come to the frontier long before those latecomers with their law books and Bibles and big talk of taming the West for decent, God-fearing folks.

It was Jacob's opinion, and he'd never been shy about voicing it—especially while getting drunk on cheap river whiskey in Ira Webb's Bullshead Saloon in Sundance—that no man tamed the wilderness with a timid soul.

Ethan had never begrudged his pa his wild ways. He'd grown up on the frontier himself, and knew what it took to carve a living out of the harsh Montana plains. But there was a level-headedness about Ethan that was absent in his pa and brothers, an aware-ness of the changes that were coming over the land now that the buffalo were nearly gone, the wild tribes clamped down on reser-vations, and towns—little dusty, wind-scoured communities like Sundance—popping up every fifty miles or so, until a man could hardly ride out in any direction without bumping into one.

Thoughts of a changing land were far from Ethan's mind as he rode down off the bench toward the ranch. Observing the smokeless chimney above the house, the empty yard and cor-rals, he felt a trickle of sweat squeeze out from under his wide-brimmed, flat-crowned hat and run down the side of his face. He was about to lever a round into the Winchester's chamber when he heard a whoop from inside the adobe house, and his shoul-ders sagged with relief when his youngest brother, Ben, came bounding out the door.

"Ethan!" he shouted, as loud and rowdy as a young bull moose. Ben was fourteen, tall and gangling, with the Wilders' pale blue eyes and stubborn jaw. Like Ethan, he wore denim trousers and a flannel shirt, but he was also bareheaded and bare-foot, kicking up a knee-high cloud of dust as he raced across the yard to his brother's side.

"Dang it, where ya been?" he called while still some distance away.

"I reckon you know where I've been," Ethan replied, reining toward the low barn.

Eyeing the mule, Ben whistled appreciatively. "Looks like you got a pack full, for a fact."

There was a howl from behind the house. Ethan drew up with a scowl. "What's that?"

The happy-go-lucky expression dropped from Ben's face. "Aw, that's Pa. He's madder'n hell at me, Eth."

"What did you do this time?" Ethan asked, then quickly amended: "Besides nothing."

"Not enough for the thrashing he wants to give me."

Dismounting, Ethan leaned his rifle against the front of the barn, dropped his reins over the top rail of the corral. His scowl deepened as he studied the house. From the sounds Jacob Wilder was making, there wasn't much doubt he was in a deadly mood. What puzzled Ethan was that he hadn't come into view yet. "From the way he's hollering, I'd say you'd better tell me what you did real fast. Maybe I can talk some sense into him before he gets his hands on a buggy whip."

"I already hid the buggy whips," Ben said. "Not that I figure that'll slow him down much. Fighty as he's feelin', he'll likely skin me from neck to heels with a willow switch."

"Ben," Ethan said with quiet impatience.

"Aw, hell, Ethan, it wasn't that much. Pa bought hisself a neat little rifle, a Thirty-Two pump, and he caught me using it to shoot flies off the ceiling in the kitchen."

Ethan swore under his breath, feeling as if a weighted harness had been dropped over his shoulders. It was just like Ben to do something so damned irresponsible, like his pa, too, to over react.

And my luck as well, he thought irritably, *to come home just in time to get caught in the middle of it.*

"It ain't the holes in the ceiling that's riled him up so much," Ben explained. "It was me using his rifle and shooting up all his ammunition. I'd've bought him another box of cartridges the next time I got to town, but that wasn't good enough. He was determined to teach me a lesson about taking another man's gun without permission."

4

"You ought to have known better in the first place," Ethan said. "You know how touchy Pa is about his firearms."

"He is almighty roused, for a fact," Ben agreed. "That's why I took off for the river before he could grab me. Figured he'd beat me black and blue if I didn't." Then a grin lit up his face like a full moon. "But, man, Ethan, that little rifle is sweet. You could shoot tin cans off a fence rail at fifty yards with that thing all day long."

Ethan didn't reply. Pa was still hollering from the rear of the house, his voice growing steadily angrier, yet coming no closer. "Where's he at?"

Ben ducked his head as if embarrassed. "In the privy."

"The privy!"

"It was after supper and Pa'd been drinking and cussing somethin' fierce, so, when he went into the privy to take a crap, I got a rope and tied him in."

"You damn', dumb . . ." Ethan's train of thought faltered. "You say you tied him in the privy after supper? Last night?"

Ben nodded sheepishly. "He's been howlin' what he's gonna do to me ever since. He's mad, Eth. Madder'n I've ever seen him." For the first time, Ben looked truly remorseful. "I guess I really grabbed the bear by the balls this time, huh?"

Ethan shook his head ruefully. They'd all pulled some bone-headed stunts over the years—Ben wasn't the first one Jacob Wilder had caught sniping flies off the kitchen ceiling—but he couldn't remember anything this bad. Ben was right. When Pa was released, he was going to pound the stuffing out of his youngest son, and Ethan wasn't sure he could stop it. Not short of whacking the old man over the head with an axe handle.

"What am I gonna do, Ethan?"

"Where are your brothers?"

"Vic took a string of horses up to Medicine Hat to sell to the Mounties. Joel's been in Sundance all week. I think he's got a girl there, but he wouldn't tell me anything about her."

5

"All right, pack up enough grub and gear to last a couple of weeks, then head up to the lean-to where we hunt elk in the fall. Stay there until I come for you, understand?"

Ben hesitated, clearly not wanting to go, but he finally nodded. "If that's what I've gotta do."

"It is if you don't want Pa whaling the tar out of you." Ethan gave him a shove. "Go on, saddle your horse. I'll pack some grub."

Ben jogged off, and Ethan headed for the house. He left his horse and mule standing hipshot at the corral, knowing he wouldn't hang around long after Ben was gone. Pa was going to be in a foul mood, and he wouldn't be particular who he took his revenge on.

The interior of the house was still pretty much as it had been when it was a fur trading post. Its walls were two-foot thick adobe—insulation for both winter and summer, but mostly protection from dissatisfied customers—its windows few and small, set up high in the walls with platforms underneath where a man could stand and fire down at those outside. The roof was sod and impervious to fire, its overhead beams peeled cottonwood, crooked and stubbed with broken limbs no one had taken time to hack off with an axe.

In the old days a counter had run down the length of the room, with some tables and chairs on the customer's side, shelves filled to overflowing with trade goods on the other. Between the shelves and racks of merchandise were two doors, one leading into the spartan living quarters of the post factor, the other into a larger storage room where Jacob had kept his robes and furs until he could ship them downriver in the spring.

Ethan could still recall the raw odors of the post—leather and hides, tobacco, bear grease, gun oil. The sounds were just as vibrant in his mind—the jingle of gew-gaws the Indians wore when they came in to trade, the pounding of drums at night, the wild caterwauling of dancers. He'd been too young to realize what he was witnessing, the loss of cultural innocence, an epochal death. To remember the land as it had been just ten years ago, and know it would never be the same again, was like an ache deep in his heart.

Jacob Wilder had torn down the counter and shelves after the trading days and used the lumber to divide the storage area into separate rooms. Although Jacob had freighted a bed in from Chicago for Ethan's ma, the boys had slept on buffalo robes on the floor—good enough for sons of the frontier.

Ethan walked from the front room into the kitchen, thinking how much the place had deteriorated without a woman's presence, a father's responsibility. Ethan's ma had died shortly after giving birth to Ben, and except for a wet nurse for a couple of years—a widowed Cree with part of her hand bitten off by a wolf pup—the place had been solely male ever since.

It showed, too, Ethan mused, staring about the kitchen. The floor was dirt, lumpy and coated in dust as fine as chalk, and the table was falling apart, its top carved over the years with all their initials, as well as some pretty artistic renditions of the female form. The heavy iron stove they'd hauled in a couple of years ago was already rusting, and dirty dishes were piled everywhere. Pulling the ill-fitting lid off a kettle sitting on the oven's warming tray, Ethan wrinkled his nose at the slowly crawling maggots inside. What the original meal might have been was beyond identification, and he slammed the lid back on in anger.

"Lazy bastards," he said aloud.

He found five pounds of flour that looked weevil-free, some coffee and salt. He shoved it all into a greasy cloth sack and took that and a tin billy and pewter drinking mug outside to set on the flat stone stoop. Then he went back in and picked up his pa's new rifle. Not surprisingly, it had been recently cleaned and oiled. Ethan knew that, if he checked the gun cabinet, he'd find all their firearms in similar condition. Jacob Wilder might be content to live in squalor, but he'd never put a gun away dirty in his life.

Hearing the slow thud of hoofs outside, Ethan returned the carbine to its corner and went to the door. Ben was dismounting from a sorrel mare, reckless grin back in place.

"I was thinking maybe I'd take some of your traps and catch me a few wolves on my own," he announced loudly. "Then I can buy my own rifle."

"How'd you carry them?"

"What, the traps?" Ben's expression became cagey. "I'd carry them on your mule."

"Uhn-uh. That mule's been worked hard enough the last couple of months. As soon as I sell those pelts to Davidson, I'm going to turn it loose for the rest of the summer."

"Hell, I'll turn it loose at Elk Camp. The grass is better up there, anyway."

"I said no, Ben."

Ben's eyes flashed darkly, but Ethan stood firm. After a lengthy pause, Ben muttered a curse and ducked past him into the house.

While Ben was in the bedroom putting together some personal effects, Ethan returned to the kitchen. There was a hutch beside the back door, a drawer under the counter where Jacob kept some of his wife's things. Opening it, Ethan rummaged through the knitting hoops and needles until he found what he was looking for, then tucked it behind his belt. When he returned to the front room, Ben was just exiting the rear of the house. He had his boots on and was strapping a gun belt around his waist, but it was the long gun clamped under one arm that brought an instant retort to Ethan's lips. "Christ Almighty, Ben, are you that big a fool to take the same rifle that got you into all this trouble to begin with?"

"I got to have a rifle, and I sure as hell ain't totin' that heavy Sharps you give me. This"—he hefted the pump .32 with a happy grin—"will do just fine for rabbits and such."

"Put it down," Ethan said flatly.

The grin faded from Ben's face. "You can't make me."

"You want to bet on that?"

Ben didn't move. Ethan could see the struggle in his face, the need to assert himself against the knowledge that his older brother was probably right, and a whole lot bigger, too.

"You're a son-of-a-bitchin' momma's boy, is what you are," Ben said finally, slamming the rifle down in their pa's rawhide-woven chair.

"You take time to sass me when pa's free and you ain't running like a scared pup," Ethan told him. "Go get your Sharps and get out of here. I'm going to cut the old man loose in a minute."

"Not yet!" Ben squawked, racing into the bedroom. He was back moments later carrying Ethan's old Sharps and a cartridge belt gleaming with ammunition. "Don't wait too long to come fetch me," he said on his way out the door.

Ethan followed, picking up the food sack on the way. Ben was already sliding his rifle into its scabbard—the long one for the Sharps, Ethan noticed. He shinnied into his saddle like a monkey up a rope. Ethan handed him the sack, then tied the billy to his saddle, but he kept the mug.

"Don't leave any food sitting around," he instructed. "There's three less bears up there than there were a month ago, but I saw plenty of fresh sign, too."

"If I see a grizzly, I'll shoot it," Ben boasted.

"It's the one you don't see that'll take your head off. Watch out for 'em."

"You're an old mother hen," Ben cried, laughing as he wheeled his horse out of Ethan's reach. He slapped the mare's ribs with his heels and raced out of the yard.

Ethan watched him go, then turned reluctantly toward the rear of the house. His pa started roaring and swearing as soon as he caught sight of him.

"Where the hell you been?" Jacob demanded hoarsely.

Ethan paused at the corner washstand they used for shaving and dipped the pewter mug into a bucket of creek water. The outhouse was set about fifty feet behind the main building, thankfully shaded by the gnarled limbs of a cottonwood, partially hidden by thistles. His pa's face was pressed against the ventilation hole. Some folks carved quarter moons or decorative stars in their doors for such purposes. Jacob Wilder had created his with half a dozen rounds from a Colt .45, then knocked out what was left with a hammer.

"Looks like you got yourself in a hell of a pickle," Ethan remarked as he handed his pa the mug of water through the ragged ventilation hole.

Grabbing the mug, Jacob drained it in two long, slurping gulps. "Jesus," he gasped, lowering his head and belching loudly. "I'm too dry to spit and too withered to stand. Cut this rope, boy. I got business to attend to."

"Ben?"

"That whelp's gone too far this time. I'm gonna peel him, Ethan, soon as I get my fill of something cold to drink."

"That's what I figured, but I can't let you do it."

Jacob cocked a brow questioningly. "You reckon to stop me?"

"I'm not even going to try." Reaching for the object in his belt, Ethan handed it through the ventilation hole.

"What the hell's this?" Jacob exclaimed, but Ethan knew he'd already recognized it.

"It's Ma's old butter knife. You can use it to cut yourself free."

Jacob's curses exploded from the privy like the shriek of a dull saw biting into wood. Ethan waited for it to taper off, then said: "I sent Ben over to Gerard's until you cool off. While you're hacking away at that reata with a butter knife, I'm going to town and sell my pelts."

"Boy," Jacob growled low in his throat, "you draw that Bowie of yours and cut me loose, or I'll hunt you both down and beat the crap out of you. And you know I'm gonna find you. Montana ain't big enough to hide a couple of pups like you 'n' Ben."

Ethan sighed. "I reckon that's what you'll have to do, then," he said, turning away.

"Boy!"

Ethan stopped but didn't look around.

"By, God," Jacob grated. "If this knife was sharp enough, I'd throw it at your yellow spine just to see if it'd stick."

"I expect you would," Ethan admitted. "That's why I gave it to you." He walked back around the house.

The bay was still standing at the corral, the mule beside, long ears flagging in the afternoon heat. Stepping wearily into his saddle, Ethan reined toward the trail that led back to the top of the bluff, the mule following docilely.

Chapter Two

Barely ten years settled, the town of Sundance was already showing the effects of a constant high plains wind and half a score of harsh Montana winters. It lay on the prairie like a scrap of cloth dropped by a passing zephyr, curved around the east side of a knoll called Cemetery Hill.

The graves had been there first—five oblong rips in the sod, halfway to the top. The O'Keefe family—father, mother, three sons. They'd been bound for the gold fields, became lost, then froze to death. At least that was the conclusion of the men who'd found them the following spring—old Gerard Turcotte and Jacob Wilder and Jacob's oldest.

Ethan had helped dig the graves, solemn of eye but hardly shocked by the brutality of the deaths, the unfairness of such loss. Theirs hadn't been the first graves he'd helped dig.

There hadn't been much to salvage, and no one wanted the dilapidated wagon or wolf-chewed harness, so they'd left everything where it lay. Later that summer, a man named Ira Webb used the lumber from the wagon to build a dugout on the leeward side of the hill. He established a store to serve the area's hunters, but also carried a few items that might appeal to a settler—lamps, milk buckets, and the like. People passed. A few stopped but none stayed until the cattlemen started drifting in with Texas dust in the creases of their clothing. The grass here was rich, water plentiful in the rivers and creeks that flowed out of the Rockies to the west. With half a dozen cattle ranches within a hundred-mile radius, the town's roots finally began to take hold.

In 1878, the ninety-plus residents of the community decided to call their town Sundance, and a delegation had been sent to Helena to apply for a charter and a post office. Five years later, the town's population had doubled, and there was even talk of someday enticing the St. Paul, Minneapolis & Manitoba Railroad to build a spur line into town. Ira Webb's old dugout had been turned into a community icehouse, and streets had been scraped out of the sod like a giant game of tic-tac-toe.

Sundance's survival, and its growth, had always amazed Ethan, who still vividly recalled the emptiness of the land on the day they'd buried the O'Keefes. He kept expecting to ride in someday to discover the whole town gone, citizens and buildings alike swept away on the wind, only the hill and its lonely graves remaining.

It was still light out when Ethan rode into town, although the sun had already made its descent behind the Rockies. He kept the bay to a lazy, dust-scuffing jog as he made his way down the center of Hide Street, its name an irritating reminder to a lot of the newer citizens of a time when hunters and traders had ruled over this region of Montana. Cemetery and Culver Streets ran east and west, and a narrow track, little more than an alley, ran north and south to parallel Hide Street on the west.

Sam Davidson was just closing up shop when Ethan reined in at the mercantile. The storekeeper paused with one hand on the CLOSED sign, his expression hardening. His gaze shifted briefly to the mule and its load of pelts, and he grudgingly jerked a thumb toward the rear of the building. Ethan nodded and rode into the alley beside the store. Davidson met him on the loading dock out back. Dipping his chin coolly, he said: "Wilder."

Ethan hesitated with his right foot already loosened in its stirrup. "Sam," he replied cautiously. "How've you been?"

Davidson was staring at Ethan's mule. "Those hides aren't going to bring much, this time of year."

"Probably not," Ethan agreed, dismounting. "But I wanted to get away for a spell, and figured I might as well make some money while I was at it. These are summer pelts, all right, but taken up high, near the Continental Divide."

Davidson glanced suspiciously at Ethan. "You've been away?"

"Nearly two months." After a moment, he added: "What's going on, Sam?"

"Aw, hell, nothing that's any of my business. Besides," he sniffed, acting embarrassed, "you always were the sensible one."

"The sensible what? You're talking in circles."

"Then maybe I ought to shut up and take a look at those skins. You say you trapped these up high?"

"Near timberline."

"That's up there, all right. Much snow on the ground yet?"

"A fair amount for as hot as it's been down here all summer." He loosened the near-side pack and heaved it onto the dock at Davidson's feet. He knew the storekeeper had changed the subject, but was too tired to care why.

Davidson cut the leather thong holding the hides together, and the bale sprang open. He started to rifle through the pack, then suddenly stopped, eyes widened. "Damn," he said softly, dragging a hide easily ten times the size of those around it to the side. "Where'd you get this grizzly?"

"Same place I got the wolves," Ethan replied, rolling the second bale off his shoulder, onto the dock. "There're two more in this pack, but they aren't for sale."

Davidson ran his fingers through the long shoulder hair. Several strands pulled loose, sticking to his hand. "Just as well, I guess, but if this was winter prime, I'd offer you fifty dollars for it."

"If it was winter prime, I'd want seventy-five." Ethan replied, grinning.

Davidson dropped the bear hide, picked up a wolf. "Well, you know there isn't any market for summer hides, but the Cattlemen's Association will pay you a three-dollar bounty on your wolf skins. They don't care how poor the pelts are as long as it gets rid of a few more calf killers."

"Three dollars apiece suits me."

"Then throw these hides inside the storeroom, and I'll get your cash and a receipt."

It took only minutes to complete the transaction. Returning to the alley, Ethan straddled the bay, grabbed the mule's lead rope. No one was around when he rode inside Palmer's Livery, so he stabled the animals on his own, rubbed them down with a burlap sack to dry their sweaty backs, then fed them and made sure their water buckets were full. Leaving four bits on the hostler's desk, he went back outside, arching his spine against the stiffness of muscles attached too long to a saddle. It was full dark now, the street nearly deserted, the night air chilly after the heat of the day.

Several businesses were still open, but it was Ira Webb's Bullshead Saloon—run-down and wind-scoured, but swank compared to the dugout he'd started in—that caught Ethan's eye. A weary smile flickered across his face. He was tired, but not that tired.

It was quiet inside the Bullshead, too, and Ethan wondered what day it was. He'd lost track in the mountains, where time didn't have the same meaning as it did down here.

Besides Ira standing on the sober side of a plain bar, there were only two other people in the saloon when Ethan walked in. One was a stranger, sitting at a table near the back wall. The other was Tim Palmer, who owned the livery where Ethan had just stabled his animals. Palmer and Ira were standing hunched over the bar in private conversation, but Ira grinned a welcome when he saw Ethan.

"Well, hell, look what the wind blowed in!" the bartender hollered, voice rumbling down the bar like loose bricks.

Palmer's expression didn't change. He stepped back as Ethan approached, as if afraid of catching something contagious.

"Howdy, Ira . . . Tim," Ethan greeted.

Pushing away from the bar, Palmer said: "We can finish this later." He stepped wide around Ethan and walked to the door.

Pausing there, staring at the street, he said: "Where's your horse, Wilder?"

"I put my horse and a mule up in that back stall of yours. I left my money on your desk. Fifty cents, right?"

Palmer turned slowly, his mouth working as if trying to form words in a foreign language. Then he just shook his head and stalked out the door.

"What the hell's he so prickly about?" Ethan asked.

"Aw, hell, Palmer was born with a burr up his ass. Ain't nobody yet figured out how to pry it loose."

"I've never seen him that way before."

"I have," Ira said dismissingly. Reaching under the bar, he brought out a quart of Kentucky bourbon. "Come on and have a snort of good stuff. It's too damn' quiet in here."

Slowly, stung by Palmer's reaction, Ethan leaned into the bar. "What's everyone so touchy about?" he asked, then briefly related his experience with Davidson, before the storekeeper found out Ethan had been in the mountains trapping most of the summer.

Ira poured two glasses to the top, then corked the bottle and put it away. He stared at the slowly swirling liquor for a moment, then picked it up and took a long sip. Lowering the glass, he said: "Folks is uneasy lately. Been some killings down south nobody knows much about, but . . . well, I reckon it's Joel that's got Tim and Sam so riled up."

"Joel? My Joel?"

"One and the same."

Ethan chuckled. "Hell, Ira, Joel's too lazy to rile anyone." He waited a moment, smile fading. "What's he done?"

"You know Lou Merrick . . . does handyman work around town?"

"I've seen him." Ethan felt a heaviness in the pit of his stomach. He'd seen Merrick's daughter, too, a solid girl of ample proportions, hair as blonde as corn silk, skin pale as a dawn sky.

Suzie Merrick was pretty, for a fact, and sure to attract all the attention she wanted. . . .

"Maybe he didn't do it," Ira said philosophically, but then he shrugged and added: "Lou says he did, though. Says Joel's been hanging 'round, talking bold and trying to get his little girl to walk out to the barn with him."

"How old is Suzie Merrick?"

"I believe she's sixteen."

"Joel ain't but eighteen."

"I know, but he's a Wilder, and . . . well, you know what folks think of your pa."

Ethan's lips thinned. "They thought pretty highly of him when they first came out here. If it wasn't for Pa, half this town wouldn't have survived their first winter." His anger swelled. "It was Bar-Five beef that kept them from starving, Ira, and coal from that vein above the home place that kept them from freezing."

"I've ate many a steak off of Bar-Five beef, Ethan, and was damn' glad to get it, but folks ain't so dependent on your family no more, and I'm thinkin' it kind of grates on some of 'em that there was a time when they was."

"Where's Joel now?"

"I don't rightly know. He rode out a couple days ago. Sheriff Burke went looking for him."

Ethan scowled. "Why's Jeff sticking his nose into it?"

"Hell, Ethan, I guess that's what's got folks so worked up. Now, I ain't sayin' he did it, mind you, but the night Joel rode outta here in a huff on account of Lou chasing him off, that gal, Suzie, come up with two black eyes and a whopper of a busted lip."

"Bullshit, Ira. Joel never hit a woman in his life."

"Joel's a good kid, but he's young and . . . well . . ." Ira shifted his weight uncomfortably from one foot to the other. "There's them that'll say all you Wilders are heavy-handed. Your daddy sure is, so it ain't much of a stretch for 'em to think Joel'd be capable of roughing up a woman."

Ethan's grip tightened around his glass. He wanted to deny Ira's accusation, but knew he couldn't. Not after what he'd just left back at the Bar-Five—Ben on the run and his pa having to saw his way to freedom with a butter knife to escape a privy where he'd been trapped for nearly eighteen hours. The truth was, the citizens of Sundance had no idea how rough and woolly Jacob Wilder and his boys could get when they weren't hemmed in by the niceties of civilization.

"Your pa's got some hard edges on him, Ethan. He rubs a lot of folks the wrong way. I know you're different, and maybe Joel is, too. . . ."

"No, we're not so different," Ethan said stonily. "It chaps me to remember how happy everyone was to see us that first winter, though. We gave those people those beeves, Ira."

"I know you did. I was one of 'em, and I ain't forgetting it. But a lot of these folks today wasn't here back then. They don't know how close a lot of us came to starving and freezing that year. And it saddens me to say, but some of them that were here want to act like it didn't happen. Like they're ashamed they had to take help from a man like . . . well, like your pa." After a pause, he added: "On the other hand, I seen that little Merrick gal the other day, and she surely does look like a cross between a raccoon and a duck. Her eyes are black and her upper lip is swollen damn' near past her nose. Someone hit her square in the face, Ethan, and Lou Merrick swears it was Joel."

"Did anyone see Joel do it?"

"Nope, but he was seen riding off afterward. Whatever did happen took place in Merrick's barn, where Suzie'd gone to meet your brother. Folks are whispering that maybe Joel wanted more than she was willing to give, she being a fair-to-middling Christian and all." He studied Ethan closely. "You got any idea where he's at?"

"Joel? Maybe." Ethan was thinking of Gerard Turcotte's cabin on the Marias, below the Bar-Five, but, before he could mention it, a chair scraped roughly across the wooden floor behind him, and Ira said—"Hell."—under his breath.

Ethan turned to look. "Who's that?"

"Calls himself Nolan Andrews, if you want to believe him. Drifted in here a few weeks ago from Colorado."

"He's a long way from home."

"I've heard it whispered that he was sent for, although he ain't mentioned as much to me. Passes himself off as a speculator in land and cattle, but he seems a mite too quick-tempered to be successful in such a position as that."

Nolan Andrews was a solid man. Not fat, but short and heavy. Like a boulder. He was round-faced and dark-skinned, with a whisker-shadowed jaw and heavy black brows. He wore a dark suit with a string tie and a pleated white shirt, although both articles looked well worn and were powdered with trail dust. His eyes were hooded, his pace lethargic. Leaning on the bar with one elbow, he looked Ethan up and down. "You Wilder?"

"No wilder than most," Ira replied, then ducked his head and snickered. Ethan grinned but didn't say anything.

With elaborate effort, Nolan seemed to pull himself together. He took his arm off the bar and stood straighter, and a hot-coal look came into his eyes. "You're cocky for an old fart, bar dog. It could get you in trouble."

Ira's good humor vanished. "You want another beer, Andrews? Something to take back to your table with you?"

"What I want is a bottle of that good stuff I saw you hide under the bar." He turned to Ethan. "And I asked you if your name was Ethan Wilder."

Ethan turned back to Ira. "Joel wasn't at the ranch when I passed through there this afternoon, but I've got an idea where he might have gone. I'll swing past there tomorrow. . . ."

"Yeah, you're a Wilder," Nolan interrupted, voice raised. "You're not as big as I expected, though. I'd heard you were twice the man your pa is, but, even as runty as that old blow-hard is, he's not that short."

A familiar warmth flowed up Ethan's spine, exploding at the base of his skull. He glanced briefly at the revolver on Nolan's hip, a nickel-plated Colt with pearl grips.

"Like it?" Nolan asked, sneering. He drew the revolver and held it up to the light. "Tuned by an expert. If you cocked it, you'd swear something inside was broken, it's that slick." He returned the piece smoothly to its holster, as much a show of proficiency as pride in the firearm itself. "Of course, you're never going to touch it. This gun doesn't leave my side. Ever."

"Must make taking a crap an awkward exercise," Ira remarked dryly.

A muscle twitched in Nolan's cheek, but he kept his eyes on Ethan. "Fact is, Wilder, I've been waiting for you to get back. I've got some business to discuss with you."

"What kind of business?"

Nolan tossed a silver dollar onto the bar. "Get me that bottle, barkeep?"

Ira stared at the coin as if considering refusal, then scooped it into his pocket and set what was left of the bourbon onto the bar. "Here she be," Ira said, cackling with satisfaction. "Or what's left of her."

Nolan picked up the bottle without response. "Well, Wilder, are you curious enough to hear me out?"

Ethan drained his bourbon in two deep swallows, then slapped the glass back on the bar. Tapping the rim with a finger, he said: "Pour me another one, Ira. I'll be back in a minute."

Ethan followed Nolan to his table at the rear of the room. A partially played hand of solitaire was spread out across the scarred wooden surface. Nolan gathered the cards with the same deftness he'd used handling his revolver, then sank into his chair, his back to the wall. Ethan sat down opposite him, ramrod straight, waiting. Nolan didn't beat around the bush. "I've been sent up here to acquire land for a new cattle co-operative. It's come to my attention that the Wilders own some of the best land north of the Marias. I want to buy it."

"Sorry." Ethan stood.

"Don't be so quick to dismiss my proposal," Nolan said. "I work for Westminster Cattle and Mining, out of their Bismarck office, and they've authorized me to make you a fair offer."

"No," Ethan said. "We're not interested in selling."

"You won't even listen to my offer?"

"I'm afraid not," Ethan replied. He walked back to the bar, where Ira stood grinning from ear to ear.

"Did he offer to make you rich?"

"You knew what he was after?"

"If it was your pa's land, then I'd figured as much. He's bought a few homesteads already, but all that land ain't gonna amount to squat if he can't get the Bar-Five. Your pa knew what he was doing when he bought that post and all the land around it."

The Wilders—Jacob and his boys—had filed on five tracts of one hundred and sixty acres apiece when the government opened the land up for homesteads—nearly a thousand acres of rolling grasslands. It wasn't much compared to some of the bigger outfits moving into the region, but it wasn't the land Jacob had been after. It was the water contained within the boundaries of the Bar-Five, an even score of the best sweet-water springs between the Marias and the Canadian border. With ownership of the Bar-Five, the Wilders could lay claim to better than twenty thousand acres of prime grassland.

Ira poured a fresh drink, the cheap stuff this time, and Ethan swallowed cautiously. "There's some kick in that one," he said.

"It's expected for them that don't know no better."

"You shouldn't have given me a taste of the good stuff. Now I know better."

Ira laughed. "I got another bottle of bourbon under the bar if you want to fork over some of that bounty money you got for your pelts."

Ethan smiled, but his expression had turned reflective. "I expect we ought to start branding our stock again."

"The Cattlemen's Association is planning its fall roundup next month," Ira said. "Throw in with them. It'd make it easier for everyone, and maybe get people to thinking more kindly of you boys. Part of what upsets folks so much is the way your pa acts like he don't need no one."

"He doesn't, Ira," Ethan replied. "None of us do."

Ira shrugged as if miffed. "Suit yourself. I was just talking."

"Who's running the roundup this year?"

"Charlie Kestler's been running it ever since . . ." Ira's words trailed off.

Ethan glanced over his shoulder. Nolan Andrews was coming toward the bar, brows furrowed into a gun sight above a blunt nose. Stopping several feet away, he brushed the tail of his suit coat away from his revolver.

"Maybe I didn't make myself clear, Wilder," Nolan said softly. "You and I have business to discuss. You took off before we were finished."

"No, you made yourself clear enough."

Nolan's lips drew taut. His fingers brushed the pearl grips of his Colt. But it was his eyes that sent a chill skittering down Ethan's spine. He'd seen that same look in his pa's eyes, right before all hell broke loose.

"I talked to your daddy a couple of weeks ago, and he was of the same opinion," Nolan said. "People told me to wait until you got back, that, if anyone could talk sense into your old man, it would be you. It appears you aren't as smart as people thought."

"You're likely right," Ethan replied mildly. He turned away from the bar with weary reluctance. "We won't sell, Mister

Andrews, and that's a flat-out fact, so let's cut the crap and get to it."

Nolan's eyes narrowed suspiciously. "That's bold for a man carrying an outdated cap-and-ball pistol."

Suddenly the old, trail-scarred Remington Army felt like a chunk of anvil on Ethan's hip, so snug in its Indian-made holster of rawhide and brain-tanned elk and fancy beadwork that he knew he'd never come close to outdrawing his opponent. But he wouldn't back down. No Wilder would.

"Now, hold on," Ira said in a disarmingly agreeable tone. "Ethan ain't well-heeled at all, but I am." There was a Derringer in Ira's right hand; Ethan hadn't even known he carried one.

Nolan swore softly and raised his hands level with the bar. "I would have figured you for a shotgun man, barkeep," he said.

"I prefer a scatter-gun," Ira admitted, "but too many people expect it. They don't anticipate a belly gun, and that's what gives me the edge."

Breathing a sigh of relief, Ethan walked over to lift Nolan's pearl-handled revolver from its hand-tooled holster. Backing away, he raised the Colt, muzzle up, and cocked it experimentally. "By damn, he's right, Ira. If I didn't know better, I'd swear this thing was broken." He handed the revolver across the bar.

"You think that's funny because your friend's got the drop on me," Nolan said to Ethan. "It won't feel this funny the next time we meet."

"*S-h-h*," Ira chided. "I'm trying to listen." He was holding the Colt next to his ear, cocking it repeatedly and lowering the hammer. When he handed it back to Ethan, there was new respect in his eyes. "That's a sweet pistol or I wouldn't say so. I wouldn't mind having my old hogleg slicked up like that."

Opening the loading gate, Ethan rotated the cylinder until all chambers were empty. He looked up in surprise when the sixth bullet dropped into his palm. "I don't know many people who carry a gun with six beans in the wheel. You're either mighty confident, or desperate."

Nolan didn't reply. He was staring at Ira's Derringer, silently seething. Ethan set the Colt on the bar, scattered the cartridges beside it, then unbuckled his own gun belt, and placed it beside Nolan's revolver. "I always did say a gun was a coward's way of settling an argument. Why don't you and me do this as if you've got a spine behind all those big threats?" He raised his fists.

Nolan looked momentarily stunned by Ethan's proposal. Then he laughed. "I'm going to enjoy beating the hell out of you, Wilder."

"You haven't done it yet," Ethan replied, but his sentence was abruptly punctuated by a startled grunt, and his head rocked back on his shoulders as if hinged at the spine.

"Jesus!" Ira shouted, as completely caught off guard by Nolan's swift response as Ethan had been.

Spun into the bar by Nolan's punch, Ethan grabbed clumsily for the far edge, barely keeping his feet. Looking up, he saw Ira staring at him worriedly. Ethan felt the same way. He'd barely seen Nolan's fist blazing across the empty space between them, hadn't even begun to duck aside when it slammed into his chin.

He got his feet under him and turned, fists raised warily. Nolan was smiling broadly as he closed on the younger man. He led with his left foot, both arms up with the elbows tucked tight in front of him, backs of his hands turned outward. Ethan recognized the stance. He'd seen it a hundred times before in newspaper woodcuts and on broadsheets—the classic pose of a professional boxer.

Nolan feigned a left, then shot his right fist forward like a cannonball, but Ethan was ready this time, and parried it. Nolan's brow arched in approval. He circled to his left. Ethan gratefully moved away from the bar, backing toward the middle of the floor where he had room to maneuver. Nolan followed patiently.

Ethan eased forward, fists moving in slow, erratic circles. He was looking for an opening, an edge, anything to even the odds. Without warning, he lunged forward, swinging low under Nolan's elbow, aiming for his ribs. But Nolan was too wily for such a lumbering attack. He side-stepped the blow and launched a quick, short jab of his own. Ethan staggered backward into the suddenly twirling saloon. From a long way off, he heard Ira shout: "Watch it, Ethan!"

"Trying," he muttered, swinging an uppercut that Nolan easily batted away, taking a sledge-hammer punch to his chest in return. The next thing he knew, he was on his hands and knees, staring at the thin carpet of sawdust on the floor. He could hear Nolan laughing. Or at least he thought it was Nolan. The sound seemed strangely distant, filtered by a roaring in his ears, the floor undulating in rhythmic waves beneath his nose.

"Get up, Ethan!" Ira shouted.

Ethan sank back on his heels. Nolan could have finished it then if he'd wanted to, but he apparently had other plans. Recalling the man's attempt to goad him into drawing his gun, Ethan suddenly understood what he wanted. Nolan Andrews wasn't a speculator in land or cattle or mining. He was a solver of problems—a killer, when the need arose—and he, or the men he worked for, wanted the Bar-Five. Nolan had tried to purchase the ranch legitimately, first from Jacob, then from Ethan. When that didn't work, Nolan had tried to provoke a fight. Ira had prevented gun play, but like Ethan, a damned fool, had handed Andrews a second opportunity as handily as a waiter offering to refresh a cup of coffee.

Ethan hadn't lost a fist fight since he was sixteen, when he'd gone toe-to-toe with his old man over a ruined supper of burned liver, but he realized he could lose this one, and the thought shook him badly. Growing up in a rough-and-tumble world, he knew how to fight. More important, he knew how to win. But he'd never met anyone like Nolan Andrews before. There was almost an art to the burly man's moves, like the intricate steps of a waltz or the deft brush strokes of a painter. Ethan couldn't win using Queensbury Rules; he didn't have the training for that. But he could still win. There was a way.

With a bellow, Ethan surged to his feet. Nolan laughed harshly and brought his fist down like a pile driver, a blow that could have broken Ethan's neck if it had connected. But Ethan had learned his lesson. At the last minute, he darted to the side, throwing a short, powerful jab to Nolan's solar plexus as he passed. Nolan grunted and stumbled backward, a look of astonishment coming over his face. Ethan whirled and swung a hard left that caught Nolan behind his ear. The big man reeled. Ethan struck again, spilling blood and spittle from Nolan's mashed lips. But that was all he got, three quick hammer-like blows that staggered the gunman, but didn't drop him. When Ethan swung again, Nolan threw up an arm, deflected his punch.

Ethan didn't even see the fist that rammed into his cheek. He fell back and would have gone down if not for the heavy table he came up against. Nolan pressed his attack, fists pumping. Ethan tried to block, to duck, dodge, and parry, but to no avail. His chest heaved and his lungs burned for oxygen; his feet seemed to drag over the sawdust-covered floor. He felt Nolan's knuckles bounce off a bicep. Another blow struck his shoulder, close to his neck. Two more struck him squarely in the chest, and a fluttering darkness descended around him. In growing desperation, Ethan kicked out with his foot, catching Nolan in the knee. It was a lucky strike and lightly placed, but it was enough to cause Nolan to lurch and nearly lose his balance.

Ethan retreated. Nolan followed warily, spitting blood. The cocky, confident grin was gone now, replaced by a smoldering rage. Ethan had seen that look before, too, in the eyes of predators.

Blood was dripping from Ethan's face, and sweat stung his eyes. Nolan was crowding him, attempting to draw him into the offensive. Ethan refused the bait. He knew Nolan had some trick up his sleeve, and he was determined to avoid it. Instead, he backed right into it.

Feeling something pressing against the back of his thighs, Ethan knew he'd come up against the table in the back of the room. The same table where Nolan had pitched his offer to purchase the Bar-Five.

He was trapped, nowhere else to go.

Feigning rage, Ethan leaped forward with a curse. Nolan stepped back, braced himself, then launched a right that should have unscrewed Ethan's head from its shoulders. But Ethan wasn't there. Using the same tactic he'd employed earlier, he dodged to his right at the last minute, grabbing the half-empty bottle of bourbon Nolan had left on the table as he did. As Nolan's fist whistled past Ethan's ear, Ethan swung the bottle with everything he had. The hard glass took Nolan behind his ear, felling the gunman in a deluge of broken glass and bourbon.

Gasping for air, Ethan sagged into a nearby chair. He thought that, if Nolan regained his feet now, he was finished.

"Lord God," Ira breathed, coming over with a tumbler of whiskey. "That's the best fight I've seen in many a year."

"He's been trained," Ethan panted, trying his best to ignore the twirling lights of the saloon.

"He was good, for a fact, but you slickered him with that bottle of bourbon." Ira chuckled.

"I'm glad he paid for it before you busted it over his head, though."

Ira tried to hand Ethan the whiskey, but Ethan waved it away. His limbs were growing weaker, and he knew he was about to pass out. He didn't want to do it here, though. He wanted to get outside, and tried to say as much to Ira, but his tongue felt stiff as a board and the words muddled up in his brain. The last thing he remembered was Ira asking if he was all right.

Chapter Three

He became aware of the pain first, like the far-off beating of drums. As the pounding grew louder, it became more intrusive, nudging at him like poking fingers. For a while he just lay there and tried to remember where he was and why he hurt so much. It wasn't until something moved his leg, a well-placed but gentle kick, that he finally woke up.

He was inside and warm. Bare wooden walls, a tin ceiling, the smell of perking coffee. Then a bearded face eclipsed the view, peering down curiously.

"You awake, boy?" Ira Webb demanded in what seemed like a booming whisper. Ethan winced and squeezed his eyes shut. Ira scooted one of Ethan's legs sideways with his toe. "Come on, son. Haul your butt outta them blankets before you take root."

Taking his time, Ethan rolled onto his side, then pushed himself up on one elbow. His face felt hot and swollen, and the ache in his ribs kept time to the surge of his pulse. He looked around the room. It was small and cluttered as only a bachelor could tolerate: potbellied stove in one corner, disheveled bunk in another, a table and single chair completed the furnishings, while a dirt-encrusted window filtered the morning light. Ethan lay on the floor beneath the window, a ratty quilt for a mattress.

"I got coffee and some of last night's warmed-over beef for breakfast," Ira said. "If you want better, you'll have to walk down to the café and order it."

"Whatever you've got is fine by me," Ethan replied, the words hacked out like phlegm. He stood and saw his reflection in the grimy window glass. "Hell," he grunted, then poked tenderly at his cheek, puffed twice its normal size. "What did the other guy look like?"

"Not half as bad as you," Ira replied solemnly. "He pummeled you good, boy, but you got in the last punch, and that's the one that counts."

Hazily Ethan recalled slamming a bottle of bourbon against a dark-haired man's skull. "Nolan Andrews?" he said tentatively.

"Yep."

"Where is he?"

"I dumped him out back in the hog trough."

Ethan stepped closer to the window. He was in one of the Bullshead's back rooms, but knew the hog trough well. It wasn't a feeder, as the name implied, but rather a shallow gulch behind the saloon where Ira deposited customers who drank too much and couldn't find their way home unaided. Six or eight years ago, when Ethan was just learning how to kick up his heels in a man's world, he'd awakened more than once in Ira's trough, cold and sick and swearing: "Never again."

But the trough was empty this morning, a barren scab.

"He was gone when I woke up," Ira confided, dishing yesterday's meat and boiled potatoes onto a tin plate and setting it on the table alongside a cup of coffee. "Come on 'n' grab a bite. I need to open shop."

Ethan turned away from the window. The meat looked dry and tough, the coffee floating a thin, greasy film on top. Poor doings for a hungry man, but he'd eaten worse. Picking up a piece of meat, he tried to bite off a chunk, but discovered his mouth didn't want to open that far.

"Damn," Ethan mumbled, cupping his jaw with his free hand and rubbing it gently.

Ira chuckled. "That was a fight," he allowed. "I never thought I'd see a Wilder get hammered by a dude in a store-bought suit."

"That dude knew how to box," Ethan reminded him.

"I saw that. The only thing Nolan Andrews lacked last night was some red tights and leather gloves." Then he guffawed, spraying pieces of meat across the floor. "And a suitable opponent."

"He caught me by surprise," Ethan replied irritably.

"If it had been your daddy he'd tangled with, he'd probably be missing a few pieces of hide this morning."

Ethan couldn't argue with that. Jacob Wilder had a reputation as a scrapper, and had been known to thumb out a man's eyes or break his knees if a fight started to go badly. Ethan figured he'd had the same opportunities a couple of times, but he'd held back. It was, he reflected, what made Jacob Wilder a tougher man than he was.

Ira got to his feet. "I can see it's gonna take you a while to chew your breakfast, so I'll leave you to it. Let yourself out the back way when you're done. I gotta run over to the bank before I open up for the noon trade."

Ethan nodded. "I appreciate you not dumping me in the trough alongside Andrews last night."

"Aw, hell, after the entertainment you provided, it would've been downright ungrateful of me."

Ethan forced a smile, waited until Ira had left the room, then tossed his piece of beef back into the skillet. He debated drinking the coffee, figuring it wouldn't hurt his jaw, but was afraid of what it might do to his stomach, so he poured that back into the pot, as well.

Tim Palmer wasn't around when Ethan hobbled into the livery for his horse and mule. He decided that was just as well, considering the way Palmer had acted last night. He saddled the bay first, then the mule, throwing the grizzly bear hides over the top of the sawbucks and tying them down.

The Bar-Five lay mostly south and a little east of Sundance, but Ethan wasn't going home. He was heading for Gerard Turcotte's place, about ten miles below the Wilder spread.

Turcotte had been on the frontier even longer than Ethan's pa, a company trapper early on, then an independent trader among the Assiniboines. He was French-Canadian, his father a post factor for the old Northwest Company, his mother a frail woman from Quebec who had died shortly after coming to the frontier.

Gerard had settled on the Marias about the same time Jacob had bought his old post from American Fur, back in the 1860s when both men had intended to live out their days dealing in buffalo robes and beaver skins. Back then, no one had foreseen the rapid decline of the big herds, least of all those who had made their living off the hides and meat.

Nowadays, Gerard mostly hunted and trapped, a subsistence living at best, but it kept him and his family fed and clothed. Gerard had an Indian wife named Corn Grower, and a daughter, Rachel.

It was nearly sundown when Ethan hauled up on top of a low rise overlooking the Turcotte home. He stopped as he always did and leaned forward to rest both hands on his saddle horn. Turcotte Creek ran its winding course through the shallow valley below him, shaded on both sides by a sparse forest of cottonwoods and scrub willow. Turcotte's cabin sat on the east bank of the creek, a squat, log structure with a sod roof overgrown with weeds. Smoke curled lazily from the chimney, and a small herd of horses grazed on the lush bottom grass between the cabin and the Marias, a half a mile to the south.

Ethan noticed that the meat racks were full, a trio of hides pegged out, flesh side up, on the flat ground in front of the cabin, the fatty inner tissue glowing like patches of spring snow.

The mule wandered up beside him, long ears flopping forward when it spotted the distant remuda. Ethan tapped the bay's ribs with his heels. It was an easy drop from the ridge to the valley floor. He kept his animals to a walk as they passed through the cottonwoods. Down here the sun had already set, and the

31

air felt cool against his bruised flesh. He crossed Turcotte Creek above the cabin. Splashing up the far side, he heard a shout from the yard, and saw Rachel jump to her feet from where she had been kneeling beside one of the hides. Tossing her bone-handled scraper to the ground, she raced toward him. Ethan grinned in spite of his split lip and dropped from the saddle, allowing his reins to trail.

Rachel never slowed as she left the hard-packed sod of the cabin's yard. She came through the tall grass like a bounding deer, holding her skirt high and to one side to keep it out of her way. Catching a glimpse of her bare brown legs caused Ethan's pulse to quicken. Rachel was nineteen, with a thick, black mane flowing down her back and sparkling eyes the color of black cherries. He had just enough time to appreciate the way her thin wool dress seemed to mold itself to her body, then braced himself for her assault. But instead of throwing herself into his arms as she usually did, Rachel skidded to a stop, her naked heels nearly sliding out from under her. Her eyes grew wide as she took in the carnage under his hat, the battered knuckles of both hands.

"Ethan!"

His smile never faltered. God, he'd missed her. "I fell off my horse," he said.

She reached up to trace his swollen jaw with her fingers. Then a wildcat look came into her eyes, and she said: "No, not a horse. Maybe a mountain you fell off of, no?"

Ethan laughed, and immediately regretted it. He touched his lip to feel if it was bleeding, but Rachel brushed his hand aside and launched herself against him. "Where have you been?" she demanded.

He wrapped his arms around her even as her long legs encircled his waist, sliding the palm of his left hand, the one still hidden from the cabin, appreciatively under her buttock. She kicked her legs when he did, and pushed away.

"You just got back, and already you wish to be chased off?"

"Who's going to chase me off? You?"

"I should," she charged, then grinned tauntingly. "But no, it would be Papa."

"I'd think your pa would be glad someone was showing some interest in his daughter. I bet he'd like to marry you off before winter so he wouldn't have to feed you."

"Probably he would. But to you?" She turned away, flouncing through the grass a few steps ahead of him, out of reach. "He could do better for a son-in-law, no?"

"He likely could," Ethan agreed.

Rachel's eyes flashed reproachfully. "*Bah!* You know better. Ethan Wilder is the manliest man on the Marias. Even Papa admits it is so."

Ethan knew Rachel's father liked him, but he doubted if the old hunter had ever made such a statement concerning anyone's manliness.

"Come," she said, taking the bay's reins. "Supper is soon ready. We will eat, then Papa will bring out some wine and his fiddle and we will drink and dance all night."

"That sounds mighty fine," Ethan admitted, his gaze straying to the cabin where Gerard stood in the doorway, one bony shoulder propped against the frame, a white clay pipe canted from the corner of his mouth. Ethan didn't see Corn Grower, but figured she was probably inside, putting the finishing touches on the evening meal. There were two other Turcotte children, both boys who were older and had long since left home; the last Ethan had heard of them, they were up on the Saskatchewan River, living in teepees.

Gerard was smiling as Ethan and Rachel strode into the yard. Then he saw Ethan's face, and cocked a brow in surprise. "You fall off your horse?"

"He has been fighting like a little boy," Rachel replied starchly, "but he has not said with who."

"You never gave me a chance," Ethan reminded her.

"Then tell me."

"I forget," he said, laughing and quickly pulling the mule between them. "I have some hides to trade, Gerard, if you're interested."

The old man's eyes shifted to the bundle of skins on the mule's back, widening when he spotted the long, cinnamon-colored hair. "*Sacre*, Ethan, are they what I think?"

"Three of 'em," Ethan confirmed. "A sow and two yearlings. I shot them up in the high country."

Gerard came over to brush the hair back from the sow's forepaw, exposing long, amber-tipped claws. "Ah, she is a beauty, no?"

She had been more beautiful alive than dead, Ethan recalled, and a lot more terrifying. He'd come across her just below timberline, rooting for grubs under a fallen pine. In working his way around her, he had unknowingly come between the sow and her two yearling cubs. The three grizzlies had no more meant to set a trap than Ethan had to step into one, but none of that mattered when the grizzly became aware of his presence. She'd stood up on her hind legs and roared challengingly, and the hair rose across the back of Ethan's neck. On foot, surrounded by a tangled mass of stunted, wind-blasted trees and jutting gray rocks, flight had been out of the question. His odds wouldn't have been any better mounted. A grizzly could outrun just about any horse in a sprint, and, in that scrub, there was nowhere to run.

Throat closing, he'd shouldered the big .50-95 Winchester and tried to retreat as unobtrusively as possible. He hadn't realized how much trouble he was really in until he heard the inquisitive woof of another bear behind him. It was only then that he became aware of the sow's two four-hundred-pound cubs.

At the younger bear's cry, the sow dropped to all fours and rushed him. Bracing himself against the mountain's rocky slope, Ethan fired three times into the mother's chest. The bear dropped as if its front legs had been yanked out from under it, and Ethan whirled as the more aggressive of the two yearlings charged. It took two more stubby, 300-grain slugs to the chest to drop the younger bear. When it was down, Ethan spun to face the third grizzly. That bear was watching him from the shelter of a clump of twisted juniper. Keeping his eyes on the yearling, Ethan reached blindly for the extra cartridges he carried on an ammunition belt around his waist. He reloaded hastily as the grizzly worked its way closer through the brush—stalking him.

Ethan's ribs were taking a pounding from within, but his hands remained steady as he fed the massive Express cartridges through the Winchester's loading gate. He'd barely slid the last round home when the grizzly exploded from the scrub. Its jaws had been wide, hung with strands of saliva, lips pulled back like stage curtains from its mottled pink gums. It was less than thirty yards away when Ethan got off his first shot. Despite the puff of dust and hair thrown from the center of the bear's chest, the grizzly barely slowed. Working with quiet desperation, Ethan levered more rounds into the Winchester's chamber, firing methodically.

It took all seven rounds straight to the chest before the charging grizzly skidded into the dirt practically at Ethan's feet. Its flanks heaved for breath and its front claws pawed at the ground in an effort to pull itself closer. His throat dry, Ethan had pulled the old Remington from its holster and moved around the bear's side, finishing it off with a single, well-placed shot to the head. . . .

He blinked then and shivered, and suddenly found himself back at Gerard Turcotte's cabin, the mule shifting tiredly under its load of pelts, the old trader still fondling the sow's claws even as Rachel stared at Ethan with unabashed pride.

Gerard looked up, his expression deadly serious. "You would trade this one, Ethan?"

"I'll trade all three to you, if you want them."

"*Oui*, I want them."

The grizzlies' hides wouldn't be worth much with the summer hair still slipping, but Gerard would take the claws—considered powerful medicine to the Plains tribes—to one of the nearby reservations to trade for horses. For each set of five, he would receive a good horse that he would take into Sundance or down to Fort Benton to sell for cash. It had cost Ethan less than 50¢ worth of ammunition—and maybe a few years off the tail-end of his life, he reflected—but the claws he'd brought to Turcotte would help feed the old hunter's family through the winter.

"Rachel," Gerard said abruptly, dropping the hair back over the sow's claws. "Care for Ethan's stock, then peg these hides with the other skins. You and your mother can scrape them tomorrow."

"Yes, Papa." She pulled the big Winchester from its scabbard and handed it to Ethan, then dutifully led the horse and mule away.

Gerard and Ethan went inside, Ethan having to duck to enter through the low entrance.

The cabin was a simple, four-room affair—a kitchen and front room, two bedrooms in back. The floor was dirt but swept clean and watered regularly, the low ceiling draped with various herbs and roots that Rachel and Corn Grower had gathered over the summer. There was a cabinet and chairs in the front room, a table and wood-burning stove in the kitchen. Pegs driven into the walls held an assortment of items, from root-digging tools to shotguns, heavy winter clothing to rawhide parfleches crammed with who knew what.

Mama!" Gerard shouted with a grin. "We have company for supper. Come, welcome Ethan Wilder into our home."

Corn Grower came from the kitchen, wiping her hands on a cotton rag. "So much noise from one so skinny," she chided her husband. "Do you think I did not know Ethan is here?"

Corn Grower was an Assiniboine, a short, heavy-set woman with a face as round as a full moon, skin the color of dull copper. Her dark hair—shot through with slivers of gray—was parted in the middle, the part painted with vermilion. She wore a wool-strouding dress of dark blue, with white trim and removable sleeves. Heavy earrings dangled from her lobes, and tribal tattoos fanned out from the center of her lower lip to disappear under the first of her chins; a series of dots, like black tears, ran from the corner of her left eye down under her ear, then vanished into her hair.

A normally shy woman, it was only recently, as Ethan's visits became more frequent, that Corn Grower had started to open up toward him. He knew much of that had to do with Rachel's feelings for him, and he wondered again, as he had so many times before, what she—what all of them—expected from him.

"Ethan," Corn Grower said warmly, "come, sit. There is coffee."

"Coffee sounds good," he admitted.

"Enough for two?" Gerard asked.

"Yes, even for an old man such as yourself. Sit, and I will bring the coffee. Then maybe a little special tea." She studied Ethan's face critically. "It hurts, no?"

"Some."

She smiled. "Yes, coffee, then tea to bring down the swelling. Then we will eat. You are hungry, yes?"

"Hungry enough to eat the nose off of a moose," he replied.

Corn Grower laughed and returned to her kitchen. It was a joke between them, that she had grown up where the nose of a moose was considered a delicacy. At Corn Grower's urging—and Rachel's—Ethan had tried it once and nearly gagged on the rubbery texture. He'd eaten some rough fare over the years, including raw snake one bad week when he'd been thrown from his horse in the Small Horns and had to hoof it back to the Bar-Five with a sprained ankle and nothing to build a fire with, but he'd never eaten anything that wanted to stop halfway down his throat the way Corn Grower's moose nose had.

Supper that night was considerably better than either snake or snout. Corn Grower dished up a fine stew of peas, onions, corn, and beaver tail, with fry bread and huckleberry jam on the side. As Rachel had promised, there was wine afterward, and Gerard brought out an ancient fiddle upon which he played even the most rambunctious songs with a shyness that seemed out of character for the rough-hewed frontiersman. As Gerard played, Ethan and Rachel danced merrily, and Corn Grower sat with a blanket over her shoulders, smiling with an inner satisfaction Ethan could only guess at.

It was late when Gerard announced that he'd had enough. Ethan had also grown weary of the demanding French and Métis numbers, but he had to admit that Corn Grower's magical brew of roots and herbs had significantly lessened the aches and pains in his body. She'd promised him a second mug with breakfast, and Ethan intended to ask her for it if she didn't have it waiting.

Rachel had taken his bedroll and saddlebags into the trees across the creek where he normally slept when visiting. After saying good night, Ethan crossed the purling stream on stones protruding from the water and found his blankets already unfurled, the bay and mule grazing nearby on hobbles. He flopped onto his bedroll and pried off his boots, then quickly shucked his clothes. With a spare shirt for a towel, he walked back to the creek to bathe as best he could without soap or razor. Shivering, he scampered back to his blankets. He was exhausted, but knew he wouldn't sleep.

He kept listening to the sounds of the night, watching the stars spin slowly across the heavens, until, well past midnight, he heard the stealthy approach of footsteps in the tall grass. He whistled softly, and, moments later, Rachel glided out of the darkness, bare shoulders gleaming in the starlight.

"Good Lord, woman," Ethan whispered as she slipped into the blankets beside him. "Are you crazy?"

"Why?"

"Why?" He scooted to the side so that she would be fully covered. "You didn't leave the house naked, did you?"

"Of course."

"Your pa'd skin me alive if he caught us out here like this, and he'd likely do worse to you."

"*Oui*," she replied, "he would." Then she laughed faintly and tipped her face close to his; her breath was warm, her flesh inflaming. "Kiss me," she demanded. He happily obliged.

Chapter Four

There was no fresh, healing tea from Corn Grower the next morning, no friendly smile from Gerard as Ethan entered the somber cabin. Nor was Rachel anywhere to be seen. The looks on the faces of both parents worried him, but he dared not ask what bothered them.

Picking up his rifle and hat, Gerard said: "Come with me, Ethan. There is a thing I wish to show you." He went outside, and, after an awkward pause, Ethan followed.

Rachel was just coming around the corner of the cabin when he ducked out the low door. She was leading a pair of horses, Ethan's saddle cinched to the back of a long-legged roan, his Winchester booted under the right-side fender. He didn't know if it was a good sign that his bedroll and saddlebags had been left behind.

When Rachel came closer, Ethan winced at the faint scratches on her neck, but resisted the urge to rub the stiff scruff of his beard.

Gerard was already mounted when Rachel handed the reins to Ethan. She kept her eyes down, as was proper for a young woman bringing a man his horse and weapons, but he took heart from the quick, air-breath caress of her fingers across the back of his hand. Whatever had happened that morning hadn't changed her feelings for him.

Ethan swung into the saddle, grateful for the loan of the tall horse under him.

Gerard rode south to a gravelly ford on the Marias, about a hundred yards below where Turcotte Creek spilled into the larger river, and they crossed without even getting their feet wet. On the far bank, he guided his mount into the breaks, following a well-worn trail that led gradually upward toward the main ridge. They rode silently, Gerard in the lead, until they came to a tiny flat about halfway up. The first warming rays of the morning sun slanted over them. Gerard halted, waited for Ethan to come alongside.

"Winter, she is not so far away any more, eh?" the older man said, pulling a chunk of bread from his saddlebags and breaking it in half. He gave one piece to Ethan, along with a slab of roast elk, and kept the other for himself. They ate without dismounting, staring back the way they'd come.

From here, Turcotte's cabin was hidden from sight, but they had a good view of the empty plains beyond. It was raining to the north, slanting veils stretched between dark, turbulent clouds and the distant horizon, but to the west the skies were clear with the promise of another hot day. Gerard was right, though. Winter was nigh.

Turning his gaze toward the far-off Rockies, Gerard chewed absently on his breakfast. After a few minutes, he said: "I will ask you now about my daughter, Ethan, and your intentions toward her."

The bread went dry in Ethan's mouth; swallowing it was like forcing down Corn Grower's moose nose. "I have only the best intentions toward her. You know that."

Gerard fixed his eyes on Ethan, and a chill plowed down the younger man's spine. "You defile her, yet you say you have only her best interests in your heart?"

"I didn't defile her."

"Then she is untouched? Do not lie to me, Ethan. You have not lied to me in the past. Do not start now."

Ethan sucked in a deep breath. Up here, where the air was so clean you could see a mountain range a hundred miles away, he suddenly felt like he was suffocating, drowning in his own shame. He knew he should tell Gerard that he loved Rachel, that he intended to marry her someday. Lord knew he'd thought about it enough. But was that what he really wanted? To marry a trader's half-wild daughter, tie himself down to life other than his unfettered own?

Gerard sawed at his reins, savagely yanking his horse around. His expression was furious. "If I did not know you, Ethan . . . if I did not think you would eventually do the right thing . . . I would kill you here and leave your body for the wolves." Getting his rage under control, the older man's mien abruptly softened. "You are a good man, Ethan. You will do what is right." Then he touched the butt of his rifle. He didn't say anything, but the implication was clear enough. Even for a thick-skulled fool such as himself, Ethan thought.

"Come on. I still want to show you something." Gerard started to rein away.

Ethan stopped him with a word. "Gerard, I do love your daughter. You know that."

The old man twisted around in his saddle, his visage like a hardened scab. "Love does not feed a hungry baby, Ethan. Neither does a wanderer, off trapping wolves and hunting grizzlies."

That irked him. "You've trapped and hunted all your life."

"*Oui*, after I saw to the care of my woman and children. Now, come, we have talked enough of this."

They continued on through the breaks, silent again. Ethan finished the food Gerard had given him, but it set heavily on his stomach, side-by-side with his guilt. When they finally topped out on the ridge above the Marias, Gerard turned west, paralleling the river, and Ethan jogged his roan up alongside the old hunter's mare.

"It does not feel right out here any more," Gerard said unexpectedly.

"What do you mean?"

"It feels like trouble. Like when the Sioux used to come this way to raid. But this is not the bad feeling of being watched by Indians. This smells more of white men."

Ethan glanced at him curiously.

"Men have disappeared," Gerard said. "You have heard of this?"

"Ira Webb mentioned some killings, but he wasn't specific."

"No," Gerard replied with a trace of irony. "These men who have vanished are not of his tribe. He wouldn't know about them."

"Ira doesn't have a tribe. Not unless you know something I don't."

Gerard graced the younger man with a patient smile. "There is much that I know that you will not discover until time has turned your head gray, as it has done mine. The tribe I speak of is not of blood. Ira Webb is a white man, a merchant from the East. His tribe is the newer settlers, the homesteaders and cattlemen and townsmen who come to his saloon on Saturday night to drink and tell stories. That is a tribe I do not belong to. Neither does your father, Ethan. Jacob and I belong to a separate tribe, one that came to these plains long before all the Ira Webbs. Someday, I think Webb and his kind will be pushed out, too, but not for a while yet. Not until men like your father and I have disappeared before them."

"I'd like to meet the man who thinks he's tough enough to make Jacob Wilder disappear," Ethan said.

"He exists. Maybe he lives here even now."

"That ain't likely," Ethan replied flatly.

"You live in two worlds, Ethan, yet you belong to neither. Like the half-breed of Indian and white heritage, although yours is an exile of culture, rather than blood."

"I pretty well go where I want, and I don't intend to change."

"But are you welcome there? Does the name Wilder grant you entrance into any man's lodge, or only some?"

"That's a crazy question," Ethan remarked, but he was remembering his encounters with Tim Palmer and Sam Davidson in Sundance. Of course, they'd been upset about Joel allegedly beating up the Merrick girl . . . but, still, was there any proof of his crime? Or had Palmer and Davidson been willing to judge solely on the Wilder name, Jacob Wilder's reputation?

"Your silence tells me you know that my words are true. You respect my daughter, Ethan. I see that, or I would have killed you by the river and let the current have your body. But the Webbs and the others of Sundance, what would they think of a half-breed wife, a squaw? Would Rachel be welcome in their homes?"

Ethan sighed. "Probably not, but would Ira Webb be welcome in your home?"

"For the things I know he feels toward Rachel and Corn Grower, no. The gap"—he made a quick back and forth motion with his hand—"it is too great. The distrust between tribes has a long history, Ethan. Not just tribes of blood, but of culture, language, religion. Especially religion."

Ethan was silent as he mulled that over. He knew there was more to what Gerard had told him than was obvious, and sensed that it concerned not only him, but also Rachel. But what did he care what the Ira Webbs of the world thought? Why should any of them care?

. . . not until men like your father and I have disappeared.

Ethan pulled back sharply on the roan's reins, causing the horse to toss its head, nicker its displeasure.

Gerard stopped, too, staring back with a taut smile. "You are a smart boy, Ethan. It is good that you do not have your father's ways. Maybe for you and Rachel it will be different. Come, we are here." He guided his horse onto an old buffalo trail leading toward the river.

Ethan fell in behind, the sudden epiphany of Montana's future, and his own, raging through his mind like floodwaters.

They wound deeper into the breaks, coming at last to a sheltered cove neatly hidden by a sparse grove of bastard maples. The small cabin was little more than a shack, an empty corral beside it. Ethan could tell at a glance the place was deserted.

"Old Emile," Gerard said, jutting his chin toward the cabin. "You know him?"

"Sure. Emile comes past the Bar-Five every once in a while. He gave me shooting tips when I was younger."

"Emile is a great shot. I have seen him clip blossoms off of a prickly pear at two hundred yards with his rifle."

Emile Rodale had been a beaver trapper during the waning days of the fur trade; in the years since, he'd roamed the West from Mexico to the Arctic Circle. Ethan had never seen him clip blossoms off a prickly pear, but he didn't doubt the old mountain man could do it. Emile had been an impressive shot before his eyes started to go bad.

They rode up to the cabin and dismounted. Ethan still believed the place was deserted, but the implements scattered around the yard were disturbing—an axe embedded in a stump next to the woodpile, traps hung from the outside rafters, the fly-blown carcass of an antelope hanging from a tree branch a dozen yards away. His muscles tightened apprehensively as he approached the cabin's single door, sagging on leather hinges. A spider web clung to the jamb and latch, a half-eaten fly drying in its clutches near its center—proof, Ethan supposed, that no one had been here in a long while.

Gerard hung back. "Go on," he said, indicating the door with a tip of his head.

Resisting the urge to draw his revolver, Ethan brushed the web aside and jerked the latch free. The door swung open on its own weight, and Ethan ducked inside.

Emile's cabin was little different from many of the others Ethan had seen, especially those built and used by old-timers who had spent a lifetime doing without, and figured they could end their days the same. It was maybe fifteen feet square, with a low ceiling and a single window hewed out of the wall facing the cove's entrance. There was a fireplace in the rear wall, humped with gray ash, robes and blankets that constituted a bed in one corner, the odds and ends of a hunter's life—spare springs for traps, pieces of leather for repairs, a smattering of cooking and eating utensils—scattered around, filling corners and niches. A saddle rested on its horn and pommel next to the door, a bridle draped over the rear skirt. Ethan's gaze roamed the cabin once, then came back to the saddle.

"Where is he?"

"A good question, I think," Gerard replied, standing in the doorway.

Ethan moved deeper into the room, studying the dirt floor. It was hard-packed from years of use, but layered with dust that revealed a story in itself. Old Emile's moccasin tracks created a familiar pattern; the boot prints looked out of place.

"I'd say he had some company recently," Ethan said.

"I was here a week ago, but did not enter the cabin. The fly on the latch was fresh then."

"Were there boot tracks here then?"

"Outside, *oui*. Three men wearing spurs, but no sign of trouble."

"So they were invited in?"

"Either that, or they came inside after Emile left."

"What do you think?"

"I think maybe they came to the cabin and somehow managed to draw their guns before Emile could reach his rifle. Had it been otherwise, there would be blood, and at least one dead man who would no longer need spurs."

"You figure they left with Emile?"

"I think so, yes. I think, if I had come a few days earlier, I would have been able to find Emile by the buzzards circling in the sky, but there were no buzzards on the day I came."

Ethan stepped outside, gaze straying toward the corral. "And his horses?"

"Emile was always trading back and forth. I could not say how many he had or where they were taken."

"Why would anyone want to kill old Emile Rodale?"

"That question is simple. Emile had something they wanted."

"His rifle? Horses? What else would he have had that was of any value?"

"Horses, maybe. His rifle was old and temperamental. Not many men today would have the patience to learn its quirks. But Emile never had many horses. I think it was something else. The land, maybe."

"His land? I don't think he ever filed on it, did he?"

"No, but if a man wanted this land, what would Emile have told them?"

Ethan smiled. "He'd have told them to get the hell out, before he gut-shot every one of them." His smile faded then, recalling the offer Nolan Andrews had made him in the Bullshead. Claiming he represented a nebulous outfit called Westminster Cattle and Mining, Nolan had said he wanted to buy the Bar-Five, but when Ethan refused, as Jacob had earlier, the gunman had attempted to goad him into a fight. With revolvers at first, then with fists, after Ira had flourished his Derringer. But what might have happened if Ira hadn't pulled his two-shooter, if Ethan had allowed Nolan to egg him into a gunfight?

"You are thinking of something," Gerard prodded gently.

Ethan had briefly explained his fight in the Bullshead to Gerard last night. He elaborated on it now, filling him in on Nolan's offer to purchase the Bar-Five, and about his earlier conversation with Jacob.

When he'd finished, Gerard said: "I think maybe you should warn your papa to watch for this one, Ethan. He sounds dangerous, and maybe not so honorable, no?"

"Honor isn't a word that comes to mind," Ethan admitted. "I don't reckon Pa needs to be told to watch his back, though."

"And old Emile?"

Ethan hesitated. "Yeah, maybe you're right."

"I *am* right." Gerard moved out into the cove, looking around as if for some new sign he'd missed earlier. After a while, he said: "I fear very strongly that I am right about old Emile, too, and that makes my heart weep. Come, we will go home on a different trail, one that winds through the breaks. It will take longer, but it will give us a chance to hunt for Emile's body."

"You're that convinced he's dead?"

Gerard nodded sadly. "Tomorrow, I will come back with more supplies, and I will not leave until he is found and buried. That is how convinced I am, my young friend."

* * * * *

It was after dark by the time Ethan and Gerard returned to Turcotte's cabin. Lamplight glowed cheerfully from the open front door, and Ethan could see Rachel sitting on the stoop. She stood when she heard their approach, but didn't come to meet them.

Movement drew Ethan's eye toward the creek, and he tensed instinctively. There was a man sitting in the shadows close to the water. He rose and walked over to the cabin when he spied Gerard and Ethan, nothing threatening in either his stride or Rachel's response.

"Jimmy Chews!" Gerard called, even before the stranger had identified himself or come into the cabin's light.

Ethan relaxed. Jimmy Chews was a half-breed Crow who had a cabin a day's ride west of the Bar-Five. Like Gerard and Jacob, he was another old-timer who had ridden and hunted these plains long before the first longhorn came up the trail from Texas. Gerard would have said Jimmy was a member of the same spiritual tribe as he and Jacob, and Ethan wouldn't have argued the point.

Jimmy was tall and slim, wearing buckskin trousers, a calico shirt, moccasins, and a derby hat. He carried an old muzzle-loading Hawken rifle in his right hand, its shooting bag and powder horn slung over his left shoulder. A shaggy gray mare with a full udder and a foal at its side followed him, heavily packed for travel.

"Jimmy," Gerard said with a welcoming grin. "A long time now since your shadow has fallen over my door."

"A long time," Jimmy Chews agreed, then graced Ethan with a quick, guarded nod. "Ethan."

"Jimmy."

"What brings you, old friend?" Gerard asked, dismounting and handing his reins to Rachel.

Ethan also dismounted, but he hung back, sensing something out of kilter in the half-breed's rigid stance.

"I have a debt," Jimmy said. "I have come to pay it."

"*Oui*, money for a hatchet and some tobacco."

Jimmy drew some coins from a leather poke and handed them to Gerard. "Is this enough?"

"Too much," Gerard replied, returning several coins. It was the way of traders, Ethan knew, and why some prospered and others grew rich in friends alone. "You will stay the night?"

"No, I came only to pay you the money." Jimmy returned the poke to his shooting bag, studiously avoiding looking at Ethan.

Gerard said: "Something troubles you, my friend?"

"You know of McMillan and his woman?"

"I know Ian McMillan, yes."

"He is dead," Jimmy said bluntly. "His woman, too."

Gerard's face went slack. "What happened?"

"The white man's death." Jimmy made a motion beside his neck, as if pulling tight an invisible noose. "Crazy Dog found them."

Crazy Dog was another mixed-blood Crow with a shack close to Jimmy's.

"Who did it?" Gerard asked, his expression darkening.

"It was not seen, but it is known that men came to McMillan's place and told him the land was no longer his. McMillan did not understand this talk, as he knew the land did not belong to anyone, no more than the sky or the clouds can belong to one man. But these men wanted the land under McMillan's cabin, and told him he must leave. Then they rode away. They came to my place and said the same thing. Then they went to Crazy Dog and told him these same words. Crazy Dog came to me after these men left and we agreed we would not leave. Then we rode over to McMillan's place to talk to him and found him and the woman hanging from a tree in front of their cabin. That was when Crazy Dog and I decided we would leave." A fearful look came into Jimmy's eyes. "That is not a good way to die, Turcotte. It causes the spirit to become trapped inside the body, so it cannot leave. It rots inside, and. after the body falls apart, the spirit is forced to wander the earth forever after, without home or friends." He shuddered, this man who had fought the wilderness for a lifetime, who had battled bears and blizzards and other men, yet now looked as frightened as a child who believes there are monsters under his bed. Jimmy pulled his mare close, gathered his reins above her withers. "I came here to warn you, Turcotte. Crazy Dog went west along the Marias to warn those who live in that direction. We will meet later, he and I, above the big cut bank, and together we will ride to the Grandmother's land. You should come with us."

Gerard shook his head. "I will not be driven from my home."

Jimmy nodded understandingly. "I felt the same way until I saw McMillan and his woman. Now I think I will find a new home." He stepped into his saddle, paused, then looked at Ethan. "I went past your father's place as well, Ethan."

"What did Pa say?"

Jimmy ducked his head, and Ethan's gut drew taut. "Jacob Wilder is dead. Your brother Ben was taken to the village called

Sundance, where it is said the people of that village want to hang him for the murder of your father." He shook his head remorsefully. "I do not believe this thing they say of Ben, but I don't think the people of Sundance care. I think they want to hang a Wilder, and that maybe they will hang Ben whether he killed your father or not."

Ethan swung into the roan's saddle. "I'm borrowing your horse, Gerard."

Turcotte nodded curtly. Rachel stepped close, eyes wide in fear. "Be careful," she whispered.

He nodded and gently cupped her cheek with his hand. "I'll be back as soon as I can," he promised. Then he pulled the roan around and raced into the night.

Chapter Five

Despite his hurry, Ethan soon realized he couldn't push the roan over the dark trail without risking serious injury to either him or his mount. Forced to a walk, it took most of the night to reach Sundance.

It was still dark when he rode into town. The jail sat on the corner of Hide and Culver Streets, half a block north of the Bullshead. Leaving his horse at the rail, Ethan tried the front door. It was locked, so he knocked, keeping at it until he finally heard movement inside. A moment later, a sleepy voice asked who it was.

"Ethan Wilder."

That brought a drawn-out silence.

"Who's in there?" Ethan demanded, growing impatient.

"Ralph Finch."

Finch was a warehouse man for the Diamond T Freight Company, but deputied part time when the sheriff was short-handed. Finch was a tall, gangling man in his mid-thirties, bald, perpetually flushed, prone to taking his authority a little too seriously, in Ethan's opinion. Especially with those who were easily cowed.

"Open the door, Finch."

"There's no Bar-Five brand on me, Wilder. I don't have to do a damn' thing I don't want to."

"Open the door or I'll put a brand on your ass."

There was another long silence, then the bolt slid back and the door swung inward. Ralph Finch backed away from the entrance, a double-barreled shotgun clenched in his fists.

His feet were bare, his fringe of short hair disheveled above one ear from the pillow. Ethan thought he looked scared but determined.

"The only reason I'm doing this is because Jeff said you might be by, and that, if you were, I should let you see your brother."

"Put that scatter-gun away first. Nervous as you are, you could easily pull a trigger without meaning to."

"It would bode badly for you if I did."

"It'd bode a hell of a lot worse for you when Jeff heard about it."

Finch lowered the shotgun but didn't set it aside.

Ethan stepped inside, elbowed the door shut. "Where's Jeff?" he asked.

"Sheriff Burke took off again just before dark, lookin' for that other brother of yours."

"Joel?"

"Uhn-huh. He was back again last night pesterin' Lou Merrick's little girl. Lou says he slapped her around some more, then rode out."

"That sounds pretty flimsy," Ethan said, scowling.

Finch shrugged. "It don't matter to me what it sounds like. I'm just here to make sure Ben stays locked up." He smirked, nose crinkling with delight. "It looks to me like you Wilders are about to get cut down a few notches."

Ethan ignored the remark. "Why'd Jeff arrest Ben?"

"Because Ben shot your pa. Not that anyone's especially surprised. Lotsa folks figure one of you boys should've done it a long time ago."

Ethan's eyes narrowed. "Who says Ben shot Pa?"

"He was seen running away from the crime. They heard the shot. Wasn't no one else around who could've done it."

"Who heard the shot?"

"Some fellas out there to talk to your pa."

"What fellas?"

"Some guy wanting to buy . . ." Finch's voice trailed off. "Look, they saw Ben hightailing it out the back way, guilty as all get out."

"And they could tell that by the way he sat his horse?" Ethan asked contemptuously.

"I wouldn't know," Finch replied, his face turning even redder than normal. "That's what they said when they brought him in."

Ethan could feel a helpless rage building within him. He wanted to smack Ralph Finch upside his head, to demand names and details, but he also didn't want to give the snide little deputy the satisfaction of seeing him lose control. Unbuckling his gun belt, he set it on Jeff's desk. "I want to see Ben."

Finch jerked his head toward a rear door. "You know the way," he said smugly.

Ethan gritted his teeth as he pushed through the door to the cell-block. Although it galled him deeply, Finch was right. Ethan did know the way. He'd awakened inside the Sundance jail about as many times as he had in Ira Webb's trough, back when he thought he had the world by the tail.

There were three cells along the rear wall, a lamp at the far end dimly illuminating the last cell, where Ben lay sleeping. Walking to the strap-iron cubicle, Ethan kicked at the heavy door.

Ben jumped to his feet with a squawk, blinking owlishly at his surroundings until he spotted Ethan. Then, with a whoop, he rushed forward. "Dang it to hell, big Brother, where you been?"

Ethan waited until Ben was close, then reached through the bars to grab him by his vest.

Ben howled in surprise when Ethan yanked him forward, slamming him into the iron grating. He began to curse when Ethan did it a second time. He tried to pull free but Ethan wouldn't let go. Finally he managed to wiggle out of his vest and stumble backward, out of Ethan's reach. "What the hell's the matter with you?" he shouted.

"You bull-headed, stupid son-of-a-bitch," Ethan said harshly. "I told you to head for the high country. Instead, you're caught skulking around home like a thief."

"Aw, hell, Ethan, what was I gonna do at Elk Camp? Chop wood?"

"Yeah, that would've been something useful. What did you think you were going to do down here?"

"I wasn't gonna stay. I just wanted to slip in and borrow Pa's rifle while . . ."

"You came back to steal the same damn' rifle that got you into trouble with Pa to begin with? What the hell's the matter with you?"

"Quit yellin', dang it. I didn't do nothing wrong."

"That's why Burke's got you locked up in here? Because you didn't do anything wrong?" He took a deep breath, then let it out slowly. Inside the cell, Ben's eyes were growing moist. "All right, tell me what happened."

Ben shrugged. "I was coming back to borrow Pa's rifle and I seen these jaspers poking around, so I slipped in quiet-like to see what was going on. One of 'em must've spotted me, because I heard a shout, and the next thing I knew they was all swarmin' after me, hollerin' like wild Injuns. I'd've probably got away, but I didn't see one of 'em watching from the trees. He jumped out and my horse spooked and lost its footing. Next thing I knew, these fellas was all over me."

"Was Burke with them?"

"Naw, they was all strangers."

"What did they say?"

"They were sayin' all kinds of things at first, like let's hang him and let's shoot him. Then one of 'em says no, we'll take him in and kill two birds with one stone." Tears welled suddenly in Ben's eyes. He swiped at them with the back of his hand. "I didn't do nothin', Ethan. Lord A'mighty, I never even seen Pa. They had him all bundled up in a blanket by they time they got me back to the house. You gotta believe me."

Ethan nodded grimly. "I believe you," he said, but wondered if anyone else would.

Ben started to come close, then seemed to think better of it and stayed where he was, out of Ethan's reach. "Finch says they're gonna hang me. Says them land speculators saw the whole thing, and they're gonna swear it was me, but that ain't nothing but a bald-faced lie."

"I know," Ethan said gently. "Did you see anyone after you left home, or did anyone see you?"

"No, you was the last person I saw until I come back."

"Where were you going after you stole Pa's rifle?"

"Dang it, I wasn't gonna steal it. I was just gonna borrow it, maybe take it over to the Blackfoot Reservation and show some of the boys."

"Some of the girls, too?"

Ben grinned self-consciously. "Maybe Walks-in-the-Wind. She's been smiling awful big when I ride past."

Ethan smiled, too, in spite of his fear, then tipped his head forward against the cold iron bars of the cell. What had happened to the world, where a boy couldn't show off a little for a girl and not get thrown in jail for murder?

"Ethan," Ben said softly.

"Yeah?" He looked up.

"You're not gonna let 'em hang me, are you?"

"Not if I can help it."

Ben mulled that over for a moment, and his expression gradually turned to fright. "What's that mean? You saying you maybe won't be able to stop 'em?"

"I don't know, Ben. Everything's happening so fast I haven't had time to think." He pushed away from the bars. "But, no, I'm not going to let them hang you. I'll bust you out of here before I let that happen."

"Maybe that's what we ought to do, anyway," Ben suggested.

"No, what we're going to do is wait for Jeff Burke to get back. I want to talk to him . . . see how much trouble you're really in. There're some awful big holes in that net they're trying to toss on you. Meantime, you do what Finch says, and don't give him any sass."

"Finch is a mean son, Ethan."

"That might be, but he's also the man who'll bring you your breakfast in the morning. Don't give him any reason to forget he's supposed to feed you."

Ben's eyes widened at the thought that Finch could do just that, and there wouldn't be a damned thing he could do to change it. Ethan left him like that, wide-eyed with the growing reality of incarceration, and everything that entailed.

* * * * *

Ethan waited until after sunup to go see Doc Carver. Carver's wife, Claudia, opened the door.

"Hello, Ethan."

"'Morning, ma'am," Ethan said, removing his hat.

"I'm so sorry for your loss. Please, come in. I suppose you'd like to speak with the doctor?"

"Yes, ma'am, if he's not too busy."

"He's dozing. He was up late last night, but he asked me to wake him if you or Victor came by."

"Well, it's me, and I'd like to ask him some questions if he's got time."

Short and graying, but still an able assistant to her husband's practice, she stepped aside to allow his entry. "The doctor's office is through there," she said, pointing to a door all but hidden in the shadows of the parlor's rear wall. "He'll be in directly. And please, Ethan, don't call me 'ma'am'. Surely things haven't deteriorated between our families to the point that we have to resort to such formality."

"No, ma'am, I hope not."

Claudia hesitated, then smiled. "Go on. I'll wake the doctor."

Ethan waited until she'd disappeared up a flight of stairs, then walked into Doc's office. He wasn't sure what he was expecting, but it wasn't the tiny bundle laid out on the examining table, wrapped in a white shroud. At first, Ethan thought it must be a boy lying there. Then he saw his pa's boots and hat stacked beside a pile of folded laundry, and felt something like a fist grab hold of his guts and give them a hard twist. He walked over to the window and opened it, breathing deeply of the cool morning air. He remained there, staring intently outside, until he heard approaching footsteps, then turned as the door opened.

Doc Carver was a beefy man with kindly green eyes and a harried look that seemed permanently chiseled into his face. He had been one of Sundance's earliest pioneers, and had always gotten along well with the Wilders, one of the few who would still willingly make that boast.

They greeted each other cautiously, then Doc glanced at the table. "Would you like to see him?"

"I reckon I ought to."

Doc tugged the corners of the sheet loose, then pulled it down to Jacob's waist.

Ethan felt a moment's light-headedness as he stared at the diminutive form. He hadn't realized how small his pa really was. He'd surely never seemed that way in life. The whiteness of Jacob's flesh contrasted sharply with the weathered hue of his face and hands, while the pinky-sized hole in his chest seemed to stare back blankly.

"Is that where he was shot?" Ethan asked, his voice coming out more ragged than he would have liked.

"It is. The bullet struck his heart. If it's any consolation, he probably died instantly."

"It ain't much," Ethan admitted, licking at lips gone suddenly parched.

"No, I don't suppose it is," Doc replied sympathetically. He pulled the sheet over Jacob's head. Motioning toward Ethan's face, he said: "Would you like me to examine that?"

"What? Oh, this?" Ethan touched the side of his face gently. It was still puffy, but already feeling better. He credited Corn Grower's special brew for that. "Naw, I'm fine."

"All right. Well, I'll need to keep the body here until Sheriff Burke returns, but I expect him later today. Have you made any arrangements regarding the funeral?"

"No, I just got in, but I reckon we'll bury him at the ranch beside Ma."

"I think he would've liked that."

Ethan wondered. His ma had died shortly after Ben's birth, complications from the delivery was the common belief—this was before Carver had arrived, or Sundance, for that matter—but Jacob had never said much about her in the years that followed. Her grave was on the hill behind the house, but it wasn't maintained, and the headstone was just a river rock Ethan and Vic had hauled up there on their own. They'd scratched her name on it with a nail, but their scribbling had faded over the years until a person wouldn't know it was there unless they looked close. Yet Ethan thought it was as good of a place as any to be buried, and he said as much to Doc, adding: "I'll bring a wagon in tonight to fetch the body."

"Will there be a service?"

Ethan shrugged uncertainly. "Who'd come?"

"I would," Doc replied. "Claudia and I would be honored to attend your father's funeral, Ethan. I suspect there are others in the community who still remember the assistance you Wilders gave us when we first moved into the valley."

Ethan wasn't as sure about that, but he was feeling too worn out to argue. "I reckon that'd be fine. I'll go home and get a grave dug, maybe put on some beans and fatback for company. . . ."

"Nonsense! Claudia and some of the local women will furnish food. Dig the grave, Ethan, and I'll pass the word. We'll hold services tomorrow afternoon at the ranch, if that's all right with you?"

"That'd be fine, Doc." He started for the door, but Carver stopped him.

"You'll want to bring his good clothes in with you tomorrow, Ethan. Those rags he was wearing when he was brought here are too shabby for the hereafter."

Ethan smiled. "Those rags are his good clothes, Doc, but I'll stop by Davidson's later on and buy him something better."

Chapter Six

It was a lonesome ride back to the Bar-Five. Ethan kept his borrowed mount to a walk the entire way, so lost in his own ponderings he didn't even notice when the horse crested the bluff overlooking the ranch buildings and started down the winding track toward home. It wasn't until the hollow thud of the roan's hoofs crossing the crude plank bridge over Wilder Creek drew him out of his thoughts that he realized how oblivious he'd been. Ten years ago, such carelessness could have gotten him killed— an arrow in the back, a tomahawk through his skull. It seemed odd to think that the risks were no less today. Only the weapons had changed—a bullet through the heart, a noose around his neck.

Irritated with his negligence, Ethan reined up to study the buildings. The place looked forlornly deserted, and it occurred to him that it had for some time now. Maybe ever since his ma had passed away. It was a sad realization, and it pressed heavily on his shoulders—his parents dead, Ben facing a hangman's rope.

He dismounted at the front door and peeled the tack from the roan's back, then hobbled the horse and turned it loose to graze. He was reaching for his saddle when a prickly sensation rippled across his scalp. He dropped the hulk and was grabbing for the Winchester when the front door flew open and a blurred figure rushed him.

Ethan tried to jump clear, but he was too slow. A pair of arms encircled him, the weight of his attacker bearing him to the ground. He landed on his back, the air rushing from his lungs.

Catching a partial glimpse of his assailant's face, he tried to cry out, but the words wouldn't come. He felt himself being rolled onto his stomach, and jerked his face away from a pile of dried horse manure under his nose, fuzzy gray apples breaking apart with age. Getting his arms under him, Ethan heaved himself and his attacker to the side.

"Get off me!" he rasped.

"Not till you take a bite," the man on top of him said, laughing.

"Dammit, Vic, get off!" He brought his elbow back, driving it sharply into his younger brother's ribs. Vic grunted, and his grip momentarily loosened. Ethan tried to squirm out from under him, but Vic wasn't ready to give up. He lunged, got his arms around Ethan's waist, and forced him back to the ground. Ethan slammed the side of his fist into Vic's ear, and Vic hollered and swung awkwardly, knuckles skidding harmlessly over Ethan's skull.

"Vic!" Ethan shouted. "Vic, listen! There's trouble."

Vic stopped and sat back cautiously, not yet ready to believe.

"It's Pa," Ethan said. "He's dead."

"What?" Scrambling to his feet, Vic grabbed Ethan's arm and hauled him up. "You better not be lying, Big Brother."

"I'm not. Doc Carver's got Pa's body in town. Somebody shot him."

The blood seemed to drain from Vic's face. "What . . . somebody shot him? Who?"

"I don't know. They're saying Ben did it. Burke's got him locked up now."

"Ben? Lord, Ethan, that can't be true."

"It isn't, but I expect a lot of people think it is." He picked up his hat and slapped it against his leg, raising a cloud of dust. Vic just stared, clearly having trouble grasping the significance of what he'd been told.

At twenty, Vic was the second oldest of the Wilder boys. He wasn't as tall as Ethan, or as broad through the chest and shoulders, but he was as quick and wiry as a catamount, with the Wilder's strong jaw and piercing pale blue eyes. Right now, those eyes were shot through with disbelief, the first glistening drops of grief gathering in the corners.

"That can't be," he said, lips barely moving.

"We'll sort it out," Ethan promised. Vic looked away, and Ethan knew he was embarrassed by his tears. To change the subject, he said: "Ben told me you went up north with a band of horses."

"Yeah, a string I've been working with this summer," he replied distractedly. "I got word the Mounties were looking for remounts, so I ran a bunch up to their buyer in Medicine Hat."

"Did he buy them?"

"Yeah." Vic flashed a grin. "Forty bucks a head."

Ethan whistled appreciatively. That was good money, especially for that part of the country.

If Ethan was the best rifle shot in the family, Vic was just as good, or better, with horses. He had a way with them that few others could match, and was always working a few head for market. A Vic Wilder-trained horse was a sought-after prize on the Marias, even as word of his skills were beginning to spread beyond the valley's drainage.

"I'm glad you sold them," Ethan said after a pause. "We might need every penny we can rustle up to keep Ben from hanging." He clamped his hat on his head. "Come on, let's fix some grub, then clean this place up. Doc and his wife and a few others are coming out tomorrow for Pa's funeral."

The house was a mess, thick with a male's collection of bric-a-brac, multiplied by five—tiny animal skulls and discarded saddle tack, buntings of spider webs hanging in the corners. The dirt floor was dusty and uneven, but the smell was the worst—dirty clothes, horse sweat, food that should have been tossed out weeks ago.

Ethan dropped his saddle just inside the front door, leaned his rifle and cartridge belt against the wall, then went into the kitchen to survey the carnage.

Vic followed. Lifting the lid off of an iron skillet, he turned his face away with a grimace. "*Whew!* This was probably beans a few weeks ago, but I'd rather eat those horse apples I tried to rub your nose in. I'm gonna pitch this and everything else I can find that's gone bad, then start scrubbing pots and pans."

"Suits me," Ethan said. "I'll find a broom and start knocking down spider webs."

They worked until dusk, then broke off to eat some cold roast beef Vic had brought home with him. Afterward, sitting outside in the cool twilight with coffee and a cigar—Vic had brought a box of them back from Medicine Hat—they talked about the place and what they wanted to do with it. Vic was keen to build it up, to make the Bar-Five an outfit to be reckoned with, although with more emphasis on horses than cattle.

"I've been thinking about this for a while," he confessed. "Pa was against it because he figured an Indian pony was as good as a thoroughbred, but it ain't. A lot of people are saying a mustang is too small to work cattle, and I think they're right. I want to go back East and buy a couple of good studs . . . a Walker for sure, and maybe a Trotter, then cross them with our mares."

"That'd be an interesting combination," Ethan said.

"It would," Vic replied with a budding excitement. "Eastern blood to give 'em size and a good, easy gait, and mustangs for toughness and sure-footedness."

"Or the other way around," Ethan pointed out.

"Aw, hell," Vic said, chuckling. "We wouldn't let that happen. What do you say, Eth? If all of us throw in together, give it a few years, we could end up with some of the best stock in Montana."

Ethan studied the tip of his cigar, its gray ash curving gently toward the ground. "And Ben and Joel?" he asked quietly.

Vic sighed. "I know. I guess I just wanted to think about something else for a while." He tipped his head back against the cooling adobe, his sunny mood effectively snuffed out. After a moment, he shot Ethan a worried look. "You don't figure he did it, do you?"

"I'd hate to think so."

"They never got along, Ben and Pa. Ben was always the wildest of the Wilders, and, the way Pa sometimes whomped him, I ain't sure I'd blame him for popping a cap on the old bastard." He rolled his shoulder as if in unconscious memory. "He's whomped us all pretty good, one time or another."

"It ain't a thing to kill a man for."

"I don't know, Eth. Was some stranger to do that to one of us, we'd all hunt him down."

"We might whomp him right back, too, but we wouldn't kill him. Besides, Pa was Pa, and that's just the way he was . . . at least ever since Ma died." An image flashed through his mind, his mother standing silently at the stove, head bent to her cooking, eyes averted. One cheek had been shadowed, and a frown creased his forehead. That had been just a shadow, hadn't it?

"I'd have to take your word for that," Vic said. "I was too young to remember what he was like before Ma died."

"He was a hard man," Ethan conceded. "But as far as Ben is concerned, even if he'd done it, he would have told me. He's a wildcat, but he's not sneaky."

"And Joel?" Vic asked pointedly.

Ethan shot him a look. "I guess I'd have to talk to Joel before I made up my mind about him."

Vic drew thoughtfully on his cigar, and Ethan knew they were both recalling incidents from their past—Joel lying or stealing something small. Even out of Davidson's store. Pa finally caught him at it and pounded him good with a hickory ramrod from the shotgun, but Ethan knew the beating had only made Joel more cautious in his thieving.

It was well after dark when they decided to turn in. "I'll dig a grave up beside Ma's tomorrow," Vic said as they climbed to their feet. "You can go into Sundance and fetch Pa."

Ethan could tell Vic wasn't eager to see Jacob's body, and would probably get a lot more done around the house if he stayed behind. Neither of them had ever been shy about work, a distinction Joel or Ben couldn't come close to claiming. Or Jacob, for that matter; the old man had never replaced a broken corral rail when it could be more easily patched with rawhide.

They said their good nights and Ethan went into what passed as his room, a corner of the old storeroom partitioned off with blankets. There was a window high in the wall, and he climbed onto the shooting platform under it to throw open the shutters. He stayed there a moment, looking down toward the curve of Wilder Creek that bent past the rear of the house. With the rain-starved leaves clinging stubbornly to the cottonwoods and willows, he couldn't see the Marias, but he could hear it, purling icy cold down out of the Rockies.

Taking a final, deep breath of the cool night air, he hopped down and shed his clothes. Even with the window open, he had trouble falling asleep. The air seemed thick enough to slice, and his bunk, coarse as it was—dried grass stuffed inside a sagging blue tick mattress, ropes for springs—was too soft. He tossed and turned for a couple of hours, then hauled his blankets into the front room, where he opened the door to create a cross draft. He slept better after that, but was still up before dawn, groggy and yawning.

Vic came out of his room with a buffalo robe pulled over his shoulders, hair tousled, mood grumpy. "God A'mighty, Eth, you trying to freeze me out?"

"It was hot."

"The hell it was. You've been up near timberline too long. For those of us who stayed below, it's cold." He kicked the door shut, then went into the kitchen to stir up a fire in the stove.

Ethan chuckled after him, but, when he saw his breath, he had to admit Vic was probably right.

They had coffee and biscuits, eating in silence as the day's single chore loomed ever larger before them. When they were done, Vic gathered the cast-iron biscuit pan and their dishes in his arms and headed for the kitchen door. "I'll wash these while you find the mules for the wagon," he said. "I saw 'em down near the river, under the trees, when I came in yesterday."

"I'll look there first," Ethan said, pushing away from the table and heading in the other direction for his saddle. He was barely into the front room when Vic opened the side door. An explosion, like a bolt of lightning, shook the house, and Vic was flung backward, the utensils he'd been carrying clattering across the floor.

"Vic!" Ethan shouted, dropping into a crouch as a second volley of gunfire erupted from outside. Bullets tore through the open door with angry whines, pinging off the stove, thudding into the walls. Ethan crabbed across the floor on his hands and feet and slammed the door shut, then dropped the heavy crossbar into its iron brackets. Sprinting into the front room, he barred that door the same way, then he grabbed his rifle and cartridge belt and ran back into the kitchen.

Vic had pushed himself up to lean against the inner wall. He looked pale and scared and maybe not altogether there, the way his eyes kept flitting back and forth. Dropping to one knee at his side, Ethan gently pried his younger brother's arms away from his torso. His breath caught in his throat when he saw the bloody wound in the center of Vic's chest.

"Barn," Vic croaked, a tremble racking his shoulders.

In back of the house, too, Ethan thought. Listening to the rattle of gunfire from outside, he figured there had to be at least half a dozen men out there.

Clambering onto the platform under the high, narrow window beside the kitchen door, Ethan eased a shutter open. From here, he had an unobstructed view of the barn. He saw movement inside the stables, more along the creek that curved behind the house. Cursing under his breath, Ethan ran into the back bedroom. The shutter was still open from last night, and he peered out cautiously. There were two men making their way along the creek about thirty yards away, staying to cover as much as possible. Ethan quietly slipped the Winchester's long, octagon barrel through the window. The men following the creekbed were so intent on their approach that Ethan didn't even think they knew they were being targeted as he caught the lead bushwhacker in his sights. He pulled the trigger and the big Winchester roared, spewing a thick cloud of powder smoke from the back wall. The rifle's kick was harsh, but he was expecting it, and recovered quickly. Peering outside, he saw the lead bushwhacker crumbled on the far side of the creek, where the Winchester's slug had tossed him. Even from here, Ethan could see the bright smear of blood covering his chest like a bib.

The second ambusher had already dropped from sight. Or at least he was trying to. The creekbank was low, cover scarce. Bits and pieces of the man's body were sticking out everywhere. He was shouting something to the men in the barn, but Ethan didn't bother trying to make out what he was saying. Lining his sights on the bushwhacker's hand, protruding above the near bank clutching a revolver, Ethan squeezed the trigger. The scream that rent the air along the creek was like that of a treed cougar, so piercingly shrill Ethan involuntarily flinched.

He dropped to the floor and ran into the front room to check that window, but there was nothing to see. Cover to the front and east sides of the house were minimal, and he suspected the bushwhackers would want to take advantage of every bit of concealment they could find.

The east window revealed no surprises—a chokecherry patch a couple of hundred yards away, clumps of grass and prickly pear. Jumping down off the platform, he went back into the kitchen. Vic hadn't moved, although his eyes followed Ethan across the room.

"Vic, where's your horse?"

"Probably . . . "—he wet his lips—"probably with . . . yours. Somewhere on the . . . the Marias."

"Is there anything in the barn?"

"No . . . I don't think . . ." Vic's effort to speak was taking its toll, and his voice gradually faded, then died.

Ethan watched to make sure he was still breathing, then turned back to the window. He slid the Winchester's muzzle through the shallow slot. As he did, gunfire blossomed from deep within the barn—two, maybe three men crouched back in the shadows. Ethan turned his face away from the dust and chunks of flying adobe that sprayed across the opening. He tried to picture the barn's interior as he'd last seen it. There was the tack room—empty now that they'd taken to keeping their gear in the house—stalls filled with old straw, a water barrel that hadn't been filled in years because they no longer kept their saddle stock penned up at night. Hadn't since the Indian wars had ended.

"The water barrel," Ethan murmured. One of the ambushers was hiding behind the water barrel in the barn's entryway. He adjusted his aim, aligning the barrel's location in his mind with the rifle's front sight, then opened fire, slamming three rounds into the barn as fast as he could work the lever.

There was shouting, a pain-filled scream, cursing that broke into sobs.

Then silence.

Ethan glanced toward the creek. From this angle, he could still make out the crumpled form of the first bushwhacker. The second man, the one he'd shot in the hand, had disappeared.

Swinging away from the window, Ethan shoved fresh cartridges through the rifle's loading gate. "I figure there's five or six of them out there," he told Vic without looking up. "I got one of them for sure, then wounded another. I'm thinking I may have hit a third man in the barn. Either that or I scared the bejesus out of him."

Vic didn't reply, and Ethan looked up, his heart skipping a beat. For the first time he noticed the amount of blood soaking the front of Vic's shirt, seeping through the sleeves at his cuffs.

Throat constricted in dread, Ethan went to his brother's side. "Vic," he said in a low voice. "Vic, are you awake?"

Pulling the younger man's hands aside, Ethan used his knife to slice open the shirt, then peel it back. The wound itself looked tiny, but the flesh around it was an ugly mass of swollen discoloration.

"Aw, hell," Ethan breathed, then hurried into the front room where they kept their shooting gear—reloading equipment for the rifles, cleaning solutions, grease, oil. In a latched box under the reload bench was the only truly unsoiled material in the house, several yards of soft cotton fabric used for cleaning the bores of their firearms. Ethan ripped the white cloth into lengthwise strips on his way back to the kitchen, then bound Vic's wound as best he could. When he was satisfied he'd done everything possible, he went back to the window. No one was in sight, either in the barn or along the creek.

"I don't like this," Ethan said, even though he knew Vic couldn't hear him or respond. It didn't matter. It made him feel less vulnerable, not quite as outnumbered, to speak to Vic as if he were standing next to him. "It's too quiet. I'm going to check the other rooms."

He left the kitchen for the bedroom, where he had a better view of the creek, but there was nothing to be seen. Not even the corpse of the first man he'd shot. That worried Ethan, too, knowing they had been able to retrieve the body without him being aware of it. What else were they doing out there without his knowledge?

Shuttering the bedroom window, he quickly checked the other two, then returned to the kitchen. Vic was conscious when he walked in, but unresponsive. Offering him water, Ethan spilled as much down his chin as his throat. Rocking back on his heels, he clenched his fists until the knuckles turned white. He knew Vic needed a doctor badly, that he could die if he didn't receive adequate care soon. With Jacob already dead, Ben in jail, and

Joel dodging the law, Ethan wasn't sure he could handle another tragedy.

Time passed and the day grew warmer. The air inside the closed-off house became stuffy at first, then hot and miserable. The buzz of autumn flies attracted to the blood on Vic's shirt seemed to grow louder with every passing minute, a torture almost as nerve-racking as his sense of helplessness. Vic lost consciousness sometime around midmorning, and only stirred occasionally when Ethan moistened his lips with a wet cloth or bathed his feverish brow.

It was noon when Ethan heard his name called from the barn. After hours of silence, the voice caught him by surprise. Scrambling onto the ledge, he peeked out warily.

"Ethan Wilder! Are you there?"

"Who's asking?"

"Never mind who's asking. We want to make a deal."

Ethan's fingers flexed nervously on the Winchester's forestock. "What kind of deal?"

"Come out unarmed and walk down to the river. Don't look back. That's all you've got to do. We don't want you. It's your friend we're after."

Ethan glanced at Vic. "What do you want with him?"

"He robbed a bank in Bozeman. We intend to take him back to stand trial."

Ethan tipped his head against the wall, wishing he could just close his eyes and go to sleep. Then slowly, wearily he pulled himself up straight. "I reckon not!" he shouted.

"Don't be a fool, Wilder. Whoever he is, he isn't worth dying for."

"You should've known I wouldn't believe you," Ethan returned. "You ought to know this isn't a stranger, either. It's my brother Victor."

There was no reply to that. After a couple of minutes, Ethan slipped away to check the other windows. Nothing moved that he could see, and he went back to the kitchen, climbing onto the platform under the window. Licking his lips, he shouted: "I've got all the time in the world, boys!"

It almost choked him to say it. He knew he had time, but Vic certainly didn't.

Chapter Seven

The afternoon seemed to drag on forever. Although Vic drifted in and out of consciousness, he never again fully regained his senses. From time to time, Ethan would soak a piece of cloth in water and hold it to his brother's lips, letting him suckle like a nursing babe, but Vic's fever continued to rise, and his breathing became more labored.

Ethan also kept a close eye on the barn and creek, but no further attempts were made to approach the house. He knew they were still out there, though. He could occasionally hear the quiet murmur of their conversation and, once, the sobs of someone begging for whiskey to dull his pain.

It began to cool off when the sun went down, although the coming night worried Ethan more than the suffocating heat of the closed-off house. He knew the bushwhackers wouldn't wait forever. Come full dark, they'd try something. He just hoped he'd be ready for it.

As the shadows thickened under the cottonwoods along Wilder Creek, Ethan began to grow restless. He kept moving from window to window, the Winchester always at the ready. The last, lingering tendrils of a scarlet sunset were being sucked down into the horizon, nightfall skulking in from the east, when the men in the barn finally made their move. Ethan heard them first, voices excited and urgent, the rattle of weapons being readied. Standing at the kitchen window, he eased the Winchester's muzzle through the narrow slot, hammer cocked. A face appeared at the barn's entrance. Moon-pale and fleet as a swallow, it disappeared before

Ethan could swing his sights on it. There was a thud from the creek, a splash, nervous laughter so soft Ethan couldn't tell where it came from. Then. . . .

"Wilder!"

A hiss like escaping steam, it came from . . . where?

Leaning back, Ethan pulled his finger off the trigger. Were they were playing with him, trying to jack up his nerves until he did something foolish? Dropping from the kitchen platform, he checked the other windows. Nothing stirred, and the silence brought a taut smile to his face. Were they disappointed that he hadn't revealed his position by firing wildly at feigned targets? Had they wanted him to deafen himself temporarily with his own gunfire so that they could slip in closer? Ethan had grown up on the frontier. He was no greenhorn. If they wanted a fight, they'd have to bring it to him.

There was a shout from the barn, scattered replies barely intelligible.

". . . coming!"

". . . outta here!"

"Quick, dammit . . ."

Ethan frowned, shoulder pressed to adobe as he tried to piece together something coherent. The voices seemed to be coming from everywhere—the barn, the creek, even the chokecherry patch east of the house. He heard the dull thud of hoofs and wondered if this was their next ruse, to make him think they were abandoning their siege, riding away. He didn't intend to fall for it, yet he knew time was as much his enemy as the men who had kept him trapped here. He couldn't hide forever. Not with Vic as bad off as he was.

Minutes crept past. Sweat beaded above Ethan's brows in spite of the cooling temperatures, and along with the drone of flies was now the laborious sounds of Vic's breathing, like the distant rip of a bucksaw.

"Ethan. Ethan Wilder!"

Ethan tensed. "What do you want?"

"It's John Red Bear, Ethan. I have news."

"Red Bear?"

John Red Bear was a half-blood Piegan, one of hundreds of Métis who roamed the country between the Yellowstone and Saskatchewan Rivers. Men like Crazy Dog, Jimmy Chews, even Gerard Turcotte's wandering sons. Drifters and hunters, mostly, here one season, five hundred miles away the next.

"Are you alone?" Ethan demanded.

"Very much." Red Bear's chuckle seemed as dry as Ethan's throat. "Your enemies have left. Can I come in?"

Ethan hesitated, then lowered the Winchester. "Come on up to the house, but slow. I ain't in a trusting mood tonight."

There was movement near where Ethan had shot the first bushwhacker that morning, the soft crunch of autumn grass under soft-soled moccasins. A man came out of the trees, slim, wiry, wearing a derby hat with a feather stuck in the band. Stopping halfway to the house, he said: "I am alone, see?"

"Where are the others?"

"The cowards who hid in the barn have left." Red Bear's teeth flashed in the gloaming. "I think maybe they thought the Army was coming after them."

"Now, why would they think that?"

"Maybe they heard me coming through the trees. I have extra horses, and they made a lot of noise kicking rocks and splashing across the creek."

"I didn't hear them."

Red Bear shrugged noncommittally.

"You're sure they're gone?" Ethan pressed.

"Six men rode away. Two were wounded. Another they carried across his saddle like a butchered elk. I think maybe that one was dead."

"He was," Ethan replied flatly. "Come around to the kitchen." He shuttered the bedroom window, then walked back through the house. He didn't know John Red Bear well, but he'd trust him enough to allow him inside. Because of Vic, as much as anything.

With Red Bear safely inside, Ethan struck a match and lit the lantern. Red Bear's easy smile disintegrated when he saw Vic. He muttered something in Blackfoot, then switched to English. "He is dead, your brother?"

"No, but he's hurt bad."

Red Bear nodded soberly. "I was bringing him some horses to sell. I guess he isn't interested now."

"I doubt it."

Red Bear looked up uncomfortably. "Who are these men, Ethan? Why did they shoot Victor?"

"I don't know who they are, but I'm pretty sure they want our land."

Red Bear shook his head sadly. "It is not your land, Ethan. How many times must I explain this to the white man? The land cannot be marked up and sold like the carcass of something dead. It is like the sky and the air. It is for everyone."

"You might want to chase down that bunch of hardcases that had me and Vic pinned down in here all day. I don't think they share your beliefs."

"No, I think I will let someone else do that," Red Bear said. "You know of McMillan and his woman?"

"Uhn-huh. I was at Turcotte's when Jimmy Chews brought us word. And old Emile?"

"What of that cranky bastard?"

"He's disappeared. Turcotte thinks he dead."

Red Bear reached for the latch. "I am going away now, Ethan. Maybe I will come back in a couple of months and talk to Vic, if he is still alive. I have an Appaloosa that is as good as any horse I have ever owned."

"I'll tell him you were here," Ethan said absurdly. He followed Red Bear outside. "John?"

"Yes?"

"Are any of those horses of yours broke to saddle?"

"A couple of them are, yes."

"Gentle enough for a wounded man?"

After a moment's consideration, Red Bear said: "Not to hitch to a wagon, but to stand a rider, yes, I think so."

"I'm in a hurry, and I don't want to lose time looking for my own stock in the dark. I'd like to buy a couple of horses from you. The best you've got, as long as they're broke to saddle."

Red Bear smiled. "Go get your saddles, Ethan. I will help you put Victor on his horse."

* * * * *

Coming over the last low rise south of town, Ethan was taken aback by the number of lights still burning in the middle of Sundance's main thoroughfare. Fearing trouble, he reined the Appaloosa off the road to approach Doc Carver's house from the rear.

There was a lamp in Carver's front window, but the office in back was dark when Ethan dismounted and knocked loudly on the door. Pulling Vic's horse close, he felt his brother's chest for a heartbeat. It was there, but faint. A light appeared in the window behind him, and Carver opened the door.

"Ethan!" he exclaimed, then saw Vic slumped in his saddle and hurried outside to help. They carried him inside, to the same table Jacob Wilder had been laid out yesterday.

Noticing Ethan's uneasy glance around the room, Doc said: "I sent your father's body over to Roy Manson's mortuary yesterday afternoon. You hadn't come in yet, and, with things outside starting to turn ugly, I was afraid I'd need the room."

Claudia Carver whisked into the room like a small windstorm, fully dressed but with her hair down, captured in a net at the back of her neck.

"Bullet," Doc informed her tersely, cutting away Vic's shirt with a pair of heavy scissors.

Claudia didn't speak, but set about lighting more lamps while Doc began to bath the bruised flesh surrounding the wound. He looked up briefly. "Sheriff Burke is back."

Ethan felt a clayish lump form low in his throat. "Is he?"

"He arrested Joel yesterday, has him locked up with Ben."

"Is that why there's such a big crowd out front?"

"It was bigger last evening," Doc said. "Almost a mob. Burke got most of the decent folks to go home at sunset. What's left is largely riff-raff . . . cowboys, freighters, saloon bums." He shut up and leaned over the wound. "Hold a light over here," he said.

Ethan reached for a lamp, but Claudia cut in front of him. "I can handle this, Ethan."

"Why don't you go into the front room and get some sleep?" Doc suggested. "You look like you're about to fall on your face."

"It's been a long day," Ethan acknowledged, but turned toward the back door instead. "I'll look after the horses."

He went outside and caught up the reins to the Appaloosa and the sorrel John Red Bear had sold him. There was a small barn behind the Carver house, unused since Doc kept his buggy horse stabled at Tim Palmer's Livery. Ethan led his mounts into the barn, made sure they had hay and fresh water, then walked out to the street. There were fifteen or twenty men standing in front of the sheriff's office. A few of them carried sputtering torches or lanterns; almost all of them looked liquored up and ill-tempered—a bad combination, Ethan knew.

He crossed the street, made his way past a tinsmith's shop, then down an alley to the rear of the jail. Half a dozen soft knocks brought a curt inquiry through the heavy wooden door. "Who is it?"

"It's Ethan Wilder, Jeff. I need to talk to you."

"Not now, Ethan. Come back in the morning."

"Maybe I can help."

"If you want to help, get out of town. If people knew you were here, it'd only make things worse."

"Jeff, Vic is over at Doc Carver's. He's been shot."

Silence greeted that. Finally Jeff said: "Ethan, I wouldn't open this door to the president of the Union Pacific Railroad. There's nothing I can do about Vic tonight. I'll stop by Doc's tomorrow, when things calm down. In the meantime, I want you to disappear. Right now, the name Wilder ain't all that popular around here."

Ethan took a deep breath, then nodded to himself. "All right. I'll see you tomorrow at Doc's."

* * * * *

Slouched in a hard wicker chair, heels propped on the railing of Doc Carver's front porch, Ethan dozed fitfully. The wing-back chair made a poor bed, and it was with relief that he watched the gray light of a new day creep over the town. Pushing aside a blanket from his bedroll, Ethan climbed stiffly to his feet. Hide Street was empty in either direction, the mob having disbanded during the early morning hours.

Walking around back, he knocked tentatively at the rear door. Claudia opened it instantly. "Come in, Ethan," she said softly.

Doc was sitting in a padded platform rocker, stockinged feet propped on a hassock, a shawl draped over his legs. He got up when Ethan entered.

"I'll heat some coffee," Claudia said, leaving the room as she'd entered it the night before, a whirlwind of energy.

"I don't think I could keep going if not for her," Doc confided quietly. "She's a child of the Army, you know? Her father was the post surgeon at Fort Randolph, then later at Fort Bowie in Arizona."

"I didn't know that," Ethan replied distantly, gaze riveted to the empty table where he'd left Vic last night. A tightening in his chest made it difficult to breath.

Smiling sympathetically, Doc said—"He's in here, Ethan."—and led the way through a door into a side room. There was a bed, heavy curtains drawn closed, an array of medical supplies laid out on a table against the wall. A lamp flickered in front of a polished steel reflecting plate; Doc turned it up until its light flooded the room.

Vic lay in the center of the bed, blankets to his waist, chest swaddled in bandages. In its center was a bright red stain, like a small rose pressed under the gauze.

"Should he still be bleeding?" Ethan asked in a low voice.

"No, but he shouldn't have been shot, either. How did it happen?"

Ethan told him in detail—the first thunderous volley, the long hours cooped up in the stifling heat of the house, Vic's steadily deteriorating condition. He described the fight itself, and how John Red Bear had inadvertently scared the bush-whackers off at dusk, approaching the ranch with his string of horses.

When he'd finished, Doc scratched thoughtfully at the over-night stubble on his chin. "You say you might have wounded one of them?"

"In the hand or wrist, I'm not sure."

"The hand," Doc replied. "You shot off two fingers and the thumb."

"You've seen him?" Ethan asked loud enough that Vic moaned faintly in his sleep.

"Let's move out here," Doc said, leading Ethan back to his office. He was closing the door behind them when Claudia came in from the parlor with a pot of coffee on a tray with two cups and some blueberry muffins. She sat the tray on Doc's desk and started to speak, but was interrupted by a knock at the front door. She and Doc exchanged a worried glance, then she went to see who it was.

"Something wrong?" Ethan asked.

"Not necessarily. I've had a disproportionate amount of busi-ness the last few days, and more bullet wounds than I normally see in a year."

Claudia returned with a middle-aged man of medium height, his tousled gray hair and bulldog's stubborn cast to his features a clue to his mood. He nodded to Doc, then looked at Ethan.

"You're up early."

"I came to see Vic."

Sheriff Burke nodded, turned to Doc. "How is he doing?"

"I'll leave you gentlemen alone," Claudia said, then quietly exited the room. When she was gone, Jeff repeated his question.

After a reluctant glance at Ethan, Carver said: "Vic Wilder suffered a single, small-caliber gunshot wound to the chest. The bullet struck a rib on its way in and appears to be lodged near the heart, along with several bone fragments too small to be extracted." He cleared his throat uncomfortably. "I'm afraid there's not much I can do. I'm sorry, Ethan."

A sudden roaring filled Ethan's ears, and the room seemed to tilt dangerously. He closed his eyes and took a deep breath. When he looked again, the room had stopped pivoting, yet it seemed different, every detail clearly drawn, a clarity of focus he'd never experienced before.

"Are you all right, Wilder?" Jeff asked.

"Yeah, it's just . . . he held on so long, I kind of figured . . ."

"It's the bone fragments," Doc explained. "At least two of them have pierced the heart itself. Not enough to disrupt its rhythm, but my fear is that it's only a matter of time until one of them ruptures an interior chamber. After that . . ." He shrugged regretfully.

"How much time, Doc?" Jeff asked.

"Impossible to say. Postponing treatment, then the long ride in, none of that helped his condition, even though I understand why it had to be done."

Jeff turned to Ethan. "What about the men who shot him? Did you get a look at them?"

"Not much of one," Ethan admitted, then tipped his head toward Doc. "But he did."

"I might have," Carver amended, then told Burke of his treatment of a man shot in the hand. "He claimed it was a hunting accident. At the time, I didn't have any reason to doubt him. You'd just arrested Joel and had your hands full of angry citizens."

"It wasn't the citizens who were wanting to hang him," Jeff said. "It was some of Kestler's cowboys who were yelling loudest for a rope."

"Charlie Kestler?" Ethan asked, puzzled. "Why would his hands be so upset with something Joel might have done?"

"Because Charlie's boy, Nate, is courting that gal. Or was."

"It still isn't any of Charlie's business," Ethan said.

Jeff Burke hesitated.

"He doesn't know," Doc said mildly.

"I don't know what?"

Jeff sighed. "I didn't catch up with your brother on the prairie, Ethan. It was Lou Merrick who brought him in. Lou found him in his barn whaling the tar out of that girl of his."

Ethan tensed. "I don't believe that. You're saying Joel keeps coming into town just to beat up Suzie Merrick? That doesn't make sense."

"It doesn't matter if you think it makes sense. Lou caught him in the act, and Suzie's sworn a statement of collaboration."

"They're lying."

"Don't make it worse than it is, Ethan," Jeff said. "If it was your word against Lou's, I'd be inclined to put my faith in you, but there's no way in hell I'm going to call Suzie Merrick a liar. Not the way she's been busted up."

"Thompson," Doc interrupted.

"What's that?" Jeff asked.

"Suzie's real name is Susanne Thompson. Her father was a brakeman for the Northern Pacific Railroad. He was killed in a rail yard accident several years ago. Missus Thompson married Lou Merrick just before they moved out here."

"Well, I don't see what that has to do with what happened last night," Jeff replied defensively.

Doc shrugged. "I just wanted you to know."

"It doesn't matter who her father is," Ethan insisted. "She's lying if she says Joel hit her."

"Whoever did it, it wasn't a single blow," Doc said. "She was severely beaten."

"Then it sure as hell wasn't Joel," Ethan replied stubbornly. He looked at Jeff. "What about the men who shot Vic?"

Jeff rubbed wearily at the inside corners of his eyes with a thumb and forefinger. "All right, give me some time to go home and clean up. I'll meet you at my office at ten o'clock. You can fill out a report then."

Doc picked up an official-looking document from his desk, Incident Report scripted in large letters across the top. He handed it to the sheriff.

"Thanks, Doc. You're ahead of the game," Jeff said appreciatively.

"I don't have anything about the hand wound that came in yesterday, but I'll write up a description of the guy and have someone drop it off at your office later today."

"That'll be helpful."

"You might want to talk to some of the hunters down in the breaks, too," Ethan added. "There's a few who have turned up missing recently, and Jimmy Chews says Ian McMillan and his woman were hanged a few days ago."

"I've got enough troubles on my plate as it is," Jeff replied curtly. "I'm not interested in what goes on down in the Marias breaks."

Ethan's eyes narrowed. "I thought they might be connected."

"That ain't likely, and I'll tell you something else. I don't really care what goes on down there. As far as I'm concerned, Montana would be better off without that bunch of horse thieves and wolfers."

"Those horse thieves and wolfers settled this territory," Ethan returned sharply.

"*Bah!* I'm tired of hearing how that rabble made it safe for the rest of us to come out here. It's the U.S. Cavalry that opened this land for settlement when they put the Indians on reservations. What they ought to do now is build a fence around those reservations, then shoot any red devil they catch on the wrong side of it. That bunch living in the breaks is no better. They've spent so much time with savages, they've started thinking like them."

"Gentlemen," Doc Carver broke in gently, "this is hardly the time to argue the Indian question. There's a wounded man in the next room, Ethan's father is waiting to be buried, and tempers are flaring across town. I'd recommend we focus our attention on what develops as the day progresses." He walked over to his desk and picked up the silver pot Claudia had left there. "Who'd like some coffee?"

"Not now, Doc, but thanks," Jeff said, folding Carver's Incident Report into a pocket. "Ethan, ten o'clock."

Ethan waited until the sheriff was gone, then said: "I reckon I'll be going, too."

"Watch yourself, Ethan. People are angry, and they're scared. They've all heard about what's going on in the breaks, whether Jeff wants to admit it or not. They're all worried."

"Worried that it'll spill over into their own lives," Ethan said bitterly.

"Yes, absolutely. The prospect frightens them, and frightened people have a tendency to strike out when they feel threatened. Sometimes, they strike blindly, without logic."

"Meaning Joel and Ben?"

"Exactly."

Ethan nodded soberly, taking Doc's meaning to heart. "What do you know about Lou Merrick?"

"I've spoken with Lou a few times, and I've treated Missus Merrick and Suzie for various ailments, but Claudia and I haven't socialized with them." After a pause, he added: "Let Jeff handle this, Ethan. He's got the authority and the impartiality to get to the truth."

"Jeff might have the authority, but he didn't seem especially impartial."

"Jeff Burke was out here during the Indian wars. His opinion of the different tribes and the men who embraced them, like your father, was formed in part by the things he witnessed after Indian attacks on innocent civilians."

Ethan was unmoved. "I was a boy when the Baker Massacre occurred, but I remember its aftermath like it was yesterday. Burned-out lodges, dead Indians everywhere. I remember Chief Joseph's surrender over near the Bear Paws, too, and what happened afterward. Indians didn't hold a monopoly on savagery."

Doc's shrug was non-committal. "We can argue the rights and wrongs of the Indian wars until the cows come home, but not today. All I'm saying, all I'm asking, is that you be careful. Tempers are high right now. It wouldn't take much to set off another mob like we almost had last night."

It was vexing, but Ethan felt he owed Doc that much. "I'll do what I can," he promised. "And, Doc, thanks . . . for everything."

Chapter Eight

The sun was up when Ethan walked down to the Occidental Hotel for breakfast. The woman who waited on him kept her nose in the air the whole time, and said no more than necessary when she took his order. Ethan had steak, potatoes, and onions, all fried in the same skillet, and two thick slices of bread to soak up the grease. He drank three cups of coffee with his meal, and left $1 on the table when he was finished. When the waitress tried to return his change, he told her to keep it.

"No, thank you," she replied tartly, shoving the money at him.

Ethan's pulse throbbed in his temples as he pocketed the tip and walked outside. It was much the same at Davidson's Mercantile, where he bought a new outfit of clothes—wool shirt and trousers, a union suit, two pairs of socks, and a new bandanna to tie around his neck. Sam Davidson wasn't around, but his clerk, a sallow-faced man with his hair slicked down close to his skull, had pursed his lips in disapproval when Ethan walked in, and didn't unhinge them until he was leaving.

His anger growing, Ethan went to Jenkins's Barbershop next. Fred Jenkins wasn't around, either, and the man captaining the big chair in the center of the room was a stranger. Ethan ordered a shave, haircut, and a fresh bath.

"In town for the roundup?" the young barber asked as he tipped Ethan back in the chair.

"More or less."

"Heard about the trouble yet?"

"What trouble is that?" Ethan was glad for the warm, moist towel wrapped around his face to soften his beard. It kept him from having to control his features as the young man continued.

"Some of the riff-raff from down south have been cutting up recently," the barber said. He was placing buckets of water on the stove for the bath, before mixing the lather for Ethan's shave. "A child killed his father, and his brother beat up one of our young ladies right here in Sundance. People are very upset about it. There was talk of a lynching last night, but, fortunately, our sheriff was able to stem the tide of violence. I don't know if he'll be able to do it again tonight, though."

"What's happening tonight?"

"Bad business, I'm bound to say." Removing the towel, he began dabbing lather over Ethan's beard, all the while keeping up a steady chatter. "The thing is, Nate Kestler has been courting Suzie Merrick for some months now. Several of Mister Kestler's cowboys were in town last night when this Joel Wilder fellow was arrested, and they're pretty upset about it. They sent a rider back to Mister Kestler's Lazy-K Ranch to inform him of the situation. Mister Kestler and his men are expected in town sometime today. Frankly everyone is wondering if Sheriff Burke can keep them from hauling both Wilders out of jail and hanging them, or if he'll even try. Mister Jenkins, who owns this shop, says if the sheriff is smart, he and his deputy will take a long supper tonight, as soon as it gets dark." He wiped the excess lather from Ethan's cheeks, then stood back with a satisfied look on his face. "I knew there was a man under all that brush," he said pleasantly. "Now we'll start on your hair."

"Do that," Ethan said gruffly. "And how about keeping your mouth shut while you're at it?"

Startled by the harshness of Ethan's tone, the barber set aside his razor and picked up a comb and shears. "How would you like your hair cut?"

"The same way it is now, only shorter."

It wasn't much to go on, but the barber didn't ask again. When he was finished snipping, he handed Ethan a mirror, but Ethan shoved it away without looking into it. As he climbed out of the chair, the barber seemed to notice Ethan's holster for the first time, colorful beadwork over smoky leather, and his eyes grew large. Ethan doubted if the kid recognized the design, but it was obvious he'd figured out it was Indian-made.

The bath was in a small room behind the barbershop, the galvanized tub already half full when Ethan climbed in. He shivered from the cold water until the first bucket of hot was brought in off the stove, followed by a second that was poured slowly over his shoulders.

Nodding to a small bench beside the tub, the kid said: "There's soap and towels. I'll be out front if you need anything else."

Ethan grunted a reply. He wasn't really mad at the kid, but he was glad when he left. He needed some time to think about what was going on—Vic probably dying and Pa dead, and talk now that Charlie Kestler and his boys planned to come roaring into town to pull Ben and Joel out of jail and string them up. Ethan wondered if the kid was right about Jeff Burke showing the white feather. Ethan had always liked the imperturbable lawman, but he didn't know him well, and likely hadn't made much of an impression all those years ago when he'd come roaring into Sundance himself, determined to dry up the town's whiskey supply.

Ethan finished bathing, barely cognizant of what he was doing, then dried off and skinned into his stiff new duds. His old clothes he dumped into a barrel beside the door to be burned. When he walked into the barbershop, the kid was still there, and so was old man Jenkins. Ethan could tell from the expression on the kid's face that the old man had been flopping his tongue.

"Howdy, Fred," Ethan said, tossing $1 on the counter.

"Ethan," Jenkins replied coolly.

Ethan's gaze bore into the older man's eyes. "Tell me, Fred, what do you figure the odds are of Burke holding his ground tonight?"

"I wouldn't know. I'm not a gambling man."

"That's smart," Ethan said, the words coming out hard as thrown punches. "Because I wouldn't bet on a Wilder being lynched tonight, or any other night."

Jenkins's cheeks flushed red. "That's bold talk for a man in your position, Ethan. You're alone now, or hasn't that sunk in yet?"

"Alone against the whole town," the kid added.

"Hush, Robert," Jenkins said. He was studying Ethan closely. "You ought to sell that ranch of yours, Ethan. I don't think the Wilders are going to be welcome around here much longer."

"Who would you suggest I sell it to, Fred?"

"Westminster is buying up a lot of local range land. So is Charlie Kestler."

Ethan hesitated. He hadn't heard about Kestler buying more land. Then he lifted his hat from the rack beside the front door and settled it on his head. "I'll tell you what . . . I think I'll hang onto that land for a while. I might decide I want to increase the size of my herd."

"It doesn't matter to me," Jenkins replied, sweeping Ethan's money into a tin cash box. "I'll still be here next year, cutting hair and shaving whiskers. Lord knows where you Wilders will be."

It was too early to go to the sheriff's office, but the Bullshead was open. Ethan went there instead. Not expecting much of a crowd so early in the day, he was surprised when he pushed through the batwing doors to discover nearly a dozen men scattered throughout the room. Everyone looked up when he entered, and a sudden quiet fell over the saloon.

"Have a drink, Ethan," Ira said quickly, moving down the bar.

"Maybe later, Ira, but I wouldn't turn down a cup of coffee, if you had a pot brewed."

"There's a pot on the stove in back, though it's likely cold by now."

"Then nothing will do just fine. I came over to say howdy. I didn't know you had customers."

"Holdovers from last night," Ira explained, leaning across the bar and lowering his voice when Ethan came over. "You ought to get outta here, son, and I ain't talkin' about the Bullshead, either. Get outta town."

"You know I can't do that."

Ira nodded sadly. "Yeah, I reckon I do. How's Vic?"

"He was still fighting when I left Doc Carver's. I'll be going back soon to check on him."

"Vic is a good boy. I wish him well."

"I'll tell him you said that, if . . . you know."

"Yeah." Ira's gaze shifted briefly to the rear of the room, where half a dozen men were sharing the same table Nolan Andrews had commanded on Ethan's first night back from the high country. "I'd bet a shiny new penny that bunch had a hand in what happened out at your place the other day."

Ethan turned to look. "Why do you say that?"

"Just a hunch. Plus, they was talkin' to Nolan Andrews last night."

"Andrews." He spat the word out like it was rotten meat. For the first time, he noticed that one of the men had a raw-looking wound on his cheek, and he recalled the shots he'd slammed into the barn yesterday, the sudden cry of pain. "Any idea who they are?"

"Nope. They's a lot of drifters in town wantin' to get hired on for the fall roundup, but that bunch don't look like cowhands to me."

"The one with the sliced-up cheek, he say what happened?"

"Nary a word. They rode in late last night and been rooted under that table ever since."

Ethan eyed the empty whiskey bottles scattered across the floor around them, the haze of tobacco smoke overhead. "Any idea what they're waiting for?"

"Nope, but I'd wager something's brewin'. The whole town's on edge." Ira hesitated, then added: "I've heard your name mentioned, Ethan. Charlie Kestler's, too. Word is that Kestler's comin' in today with his whole crew."

"I've heard the same, but the Wilders have never had any trouble with Kestler before."

A shadow fell across the door and everyone looked up, the same way they had when Ethan came in. A tall man in a sweat-stained Boss of the Plains hat peered intently over the batwings for a few seconds, then walked away briskly, boot heels beating a quick tattoo along the boardwalk.

"One of Kestler's boys," Ira said. "They's a few of 'em already in town."

"Has there been any friendliness between Kestler's men and that bunch in the back?" Ethan asked.

"None that I've seen. They was all in here last night, but they kept a good distance between 'em, and never spoke to one another."

Another shadow appeared at the door, larger this time, more ominous. The tall man in the Boss of the Plains was back, flanked by two others, the mark of cowhands branded clearly on their clothing and mannerisms. They pushed through the doors and took a spot at the bar, not far from where Ethan and Ira were standing.

"What'll it be, gents?" Ira asked, affecting a neighborly tone as he walked over.

"We'll have some coffee, Ira," the tall cowboy said.

"I wish I had some. You're the second gent to ask for it this morning."

Ethan threw a subtle glance over his shoulder. The hardcases at the back table had fallen silent, watching the bar. The tall cowboy turned toward Ethan. Although he didn't say anything, his intent was clear.

"They've got coffee over to the Occidental," Ira said without much hope. "Fresh brewed and hotter'n a July anvil."

"We'll just wait here a spell," the tall cowboy said.

Ira shrugged and came back to talk to Ethan. "This don't bode well," he said quietly.

"Maybe I ought to go. I didn't come here to cause trouble."

"That sounds like a shrewd decision," Ira concurred. "And, Ethan, don't come back. It ain't nothin' personal, I just don't wanna have to clean anybody's blood off my floor."

"I wouldn't want you to, Ira," Ethan replied solemnly. "Especially mine." He was grinning as he stepped away from the bar, but that faded when the three Lazy-K cowboys moved to intercept him.

"Where you heading, friend?" the taller cowboy asked.

"That wouldn't be any of your business," Ethan replied.

"Well now, maybe it is," a shorter, darker man with a thick black mustache said. He stood between the tall cowboy and the bar; the third cowhand was nearly as tall as the first, but skinny and younger. And scared.

"No, it isn't," Ethan said, keeping his tone mild. "Now, if you'll step aside . . ."

The tall cowboy stepped forward, instead. "Why don't you just have a seat at the table there, friend," he said, indicating an empty chair nearby. "We can wait together for Mister Kestler to come in."

"Boy, you're pushing me," Ethan bristled.

"You going to let a woman-beater talk to you like that?" one of the men in back called out.

"Ethan never touched that gal," Ira said loudly, then turned on the tall cowboy. "Get outta the man's way, Clint. He ain't doin' you no harm."

"I reckon not, Ira," Clint said, right hand edging toward the revolver at his waist.

"That's enough!" a voice boomed through the saloon, and Clint jumped and half turned toward the batwings. As he did, Ethan slipped the revolver from the kid's holster, so slick the cowboy didn't even know it was gone until Ethan slid it down the bar to Ira.

The batwings swung open and Jeff Burke strode in, hooded eyes smoldering. To Ethan, he said: "Couldn't just stay out of sight, huh? Had to see what you could stir up?"

"I came in to have a cup of coffee with Ira," Ethan said. "I didn't know there were troublemakers holed up in here."

"He didn't, Jeff," Ira said. "I'd vouch for that."

The fire in Burke's eyes seemed to dim a little. "All right, maybe you didn't know, but you do now, so git."

Nodding stiffly, Ethan stepped wide around the cowboys.

"Go to my office!" Jeff called after him. "I still want to talk to you."

"I'll be there," Ethan said.

Chapter Nine

The sheriff's office was locked, but Ralph Finch opened the door to Ethan's knock. Making no attempt to hide his disdain, he said: "The sheriff ain't here, and you ain't supposed to be until ten."

Ethan glanced at the clock hanging on the wall—a quarter of. "Ralph," he said wearily, "I'm on the frazzled end of a pretty thin rope right now. You might want to keep your mouth shut for a spell."

Finch's face darkened. "You damn' Wilders . . ."

"Yeah, I heard," Ethan cut in harshly. "We think we own the valley and everything in it."

"You don't!"

"If I did, I'd sell the damn' thing to you right now for a nickel."

Finch reared back, startled by Ethan's response. After a moment, he started to close the door, then pulled it open again. "Sheriff's coming," he announced in a subdued voice.

Ethan stood quietly to one side as Jeff came in and took a seat behind his desk. Glaring at Finch, he said: "Go over to the Occidental and get yourself a bite to eat. When you come back, Polly'll have a couple of plates ready for our prisoners. Bring them with you."

Finch nodded and headed for the door.

"Ralph," the sheriff spoke sharply.

The deputy halted. "Yeah?"

"If I catch you spitting in their food again, I'll make you eat it yourself."

Finch's cheeks turned beet red. He started to look at Ethan, then thought better of it and went out, slamming the door behind him.

Jeff motioned to a chair in front of his desk. "Can you write, Ethan?"

"Fair."

Jeff set paper and a freshly sharpened pencil on the desk in front of him. "Write down what happened out there. I especially want as much detail as you can remember about the men's descriptions. Clothing, height, hair color . . . anything and everything."

Ethan nodded and pulled the paper close. It took almost an hour to complete the report—two pages filled in solidly, front and back. Jeff sat across from him the whole time but never spoke or tried to hurry him. Accepting the documents when Ethan passed them over, he grudgingly acknowledged: "I'll say one thing for you, Ethan, you ain't afraid of work."

"I figure I'd rather dig a dozen post holes in rocky ground than do another one of those," Ethan said, nodding toward the papers in the sheriff's hands.

Jeff chuckled. "We share common ground in that regard. Why don't you go talk to your brothers while I look at this? I'll give you a shout when I'm finished."

Ethan stood and unbuckled his gun belt, dropping it on the desk. As soon as he passed through the door to the tiny cell-block, Ben and Joel jumped to their feet.

"Ethan!" Ben shouted. "Are you gonna get us out?"

Joel's cell was closer. Ethan stopped there first. "Howdy, Joel."

"Eth." There was a cocky grin on his brother's face, contrasting sharply with hopelessness in his eyes. "Ben said you'd be in today."

"I told him you were gonna get us out of here, Ethan, but Joel don't believe me. You are, ain't you?"

"Not today, Ben."

His little brother's expression crumbled. "Ethan," he whispered in disbelief, knuckles whitening on the bars of his cell. "You said you was gonna get us out."

"Let me talk to your brother," Ethan said gently to Ben. "I want to hear his side of the story."

"Have you heard Merrick's yet?" Joel asked.

"Not yet, but the whole town seems to know what happened."

"Yeah, I'll bet it does," Joel said bitterly.

"Is it true?"

"If you believe I beat Suzie Merrick, then you can go to hell," Joel replied. He backed away from the bars, lean and sinewy in a cheap black suit and scuffed, dusty boots. His hair was combed straight back from his forehead, and there was a snippet of hair across his upper lip that hadn't been there the last time Ethan had seen him. Joel's eyes were the same vivid pale blue as their pa's, but lacked the intensity of Jacob Wilder's fiery gaze. Joel was scared, and it showed.

"I don't know what to believe any more," Ethan said. "I'm not back home a week and I've got two brothers in jail and another shot and barely hanging on. Pa's dead and . . ."

"How's Vic?" Joel interrupted.

Ethan hesitated. "He's hanging on."

"Joel didn't hit that girl," Ben said vehemently, "and I didn't shoot Pa. Somebody's out to get us."

"Doing a mighty fine job of it, too," Joel muttered. "Have you talked to Burke yet?"

"No, but I will before I leave. He's reading the report I wrote about the shooting yesterday."

"Ask him about Lou Merrick," Joel said. "Then ask him about Nate Kestler."

"What about Nate Kestler?"

"About how he's been sniffing around Janey Handleman so much lately her pa's had to run him off more than once. Ol' Nate ain't all that keen on Suzie Merrick, even if she is built like a saloon whore, and Charlie's worried he's going to end up with a half-breed for a daughter-in-law. That ain't setting too well with the old man. Charlie's got high ambitions for that boy of his, like maybe a seat in the territorial legislature, but, if Nate marries a 'breed, that'll end it right there."

"Wait," Ethan said, holding up a hand. "Where'd you hear all this?"

"From Suzie Merrick . . . last week." Joel came back to the bars. "She wasn't beat up the last time I saw her, Ethan."

"They're saying Lou caught you in the act."

"Lou Merrick is a lying son-of-a-bitch. I went there looking for Suzie, sure, but I never even saw her. Lou caught me leading my horse into his barn, and threw down on me with a rifle."

"So what does Nate's interest in Janey Handleman have to do with Suzie Merrick?"

"You tell me."

Ethan didn't reply right away. Janey's father was Tom Handleman, another of the old-timers who had settled in the breaks when the buffalo disappeared. He'd married a Sarcee woman named Swan's Wing in the manner of the plains, meaning he'd more or less bought her from the girl's father for some horses, a rifle, powder, and lead. They'd had a girl they named Janey and three boys who were all quite a bit younger than her. Ethan hadn't been to the Handlemans' cabin in several years, but he recalled that, even then, little Janey had been growing into a beautiful young woman. It didn't surprise him that Nate Kestler would take a shine to her. It didn't surprise him that Nate's father would be against it, either.

"Are you saying it was Nate who beat up Suzie Merrick?" Ethan asked.

"She's a clingy one, Eth, and she wants a piece of Kestler's spread. She as much as told me that. She'll get it, too, if she can corner Nate into marrying her."

Ethan shook his head. He'd hoped talking to Joel would clear up some of his confusion, but he felt as muddled now as he had that morning.

"Ethan!" Jeff called from the front office.

Joel glanced at the cell-block door and sneered. "Better go see what that tub of bull's dung wants," he said. "While you're at it, ask him what he knows about Nate Kestler. I'd like to know where that boy was the night Suzie got beat to hell."

"I'll ask him," Ethan said. "Do either of you need anything?"

"I need to get outta here," Ben said fervently.

"I'm doing what I can," Ethan promised. "What about you, Joel?"

"See if you can slip me a bottle of whiskey the next time you come in. Being closed in like this is clawing on my nerves."

"Me, too," Ben said. "Bring me a bottle, too."

"You're too young to drink whiskey," Ethan said.

Tears sprang to Ben's eyes. "I ain't, either. Not if they're plannin' to hang me. That ain't something I'd want to do sober."

"Bring him a bottle," Joel said irritably. "He's snuck enough of Pa's whiskey over the years to know what he's getting in to."

"All right," Ethan surrendered. "I'll see what I can do."

Jeff was still at his desk when Ethan returned, leaning back in a wooden swivel chair. He looked sleepy in the warm, still air of the office. Only his eyes betrayed his alertness, the wary edge of anticipation. Jeff Burke was a man caught in the middle, and, recalling his conversation with the young barber at Jenkins that morning, Ethan wondered how much of a problem that was going to be when Charlie Kestler and his men rode into Sundance.

Jeff inclined his head toward the report Ethan had written. "A good description of what happened, but lacking in important details. A red shirt, a brown hat. That's not much to go on."

"Everybody was keeping their heads down. Including me."

"Yeah, I suppose so."

"What about the man Doc treated? The one with the mangled hand?"

"If I see anyone around town with freshly amputated fingers, I'll ask him about it, but so far I haven't seen anyone who fits that bill."

"You checked the hotel?"

Jeff acted mildly annoyed by the question. "I will, when I get time."

"What about those men at the Bullshead? Are they suspects?"

"Should they be?"

Ethan could feel his anger stirring. "Dammit, Jeff, somebody shot Vic, and somebody killed Pa. Considering the bandage on that fella's face, I'd think you'd be interested in talking to him."

"There's a thousand reasons a man can cut his face that doesn't involve breaking the law, Wilder. Find me the guy Doc treated, then I'll be interested."

Ethan started to fire back a retort, then abruptly shut his mouth. He needed Burke on his side, not antagonized to the point of turning his back on them. Pulling his eyes away from the sheriff's glowering stare, he noticed the big, framed map on the wall above Jeff's desk. He eyed it with distracted curiosity. Sundance was underlined with a red pencil, not too many miles below the Canadian border. Idly Ethan's gaze traveled along the Marias to where Gerard Turcotte's cabin was located, then on through the draws and side cañons to where Ian McMillan and his wife had been hung, where Emile Rodale was missing yet. On a hunch, he said: "What do you know about Westminster Cattle and Mining?"

If the question caught Jeff off guard, he didn't show it. "Not much. I'd never heard of them until Nolan Andrews rode in here a few weeks ago claiming to be an agent for the company."

"Andrews told me Westminster was headquartered out of Bismarck. Isn't Kirk Weller a marshal in Bismarck?"

Jeff cut him a shrewd look. "I've already telegraphed Kirk." After a pause, he added: "Westminster is owned by a corporation out of New York. Frankly I doubt if they'd be interested in a man like your father."

"Or much give a damn if he or one of his sons got shot for standing in their way."

"That's a box cañon, Ethan," Jeff said gently. "You'd easier rope a bolt of lightning as tie your pa's murder to one of Westminster's bigwigs."

"What about Andrews?"

"You stay away from Nolan Andrews. He's bad medicine."

"I've already met him once. He didn't seem so tough to me."

"Yeah, I can see he was a real kitten by the cuts and bruises on your face. I mean it, Ethan, shy clear of that one."

"You know, Jeff, no one's ever told me who brought Ben in."

Burke shifted uncomfortably. "Some fellas."

"Was Nolan Andrews one of them?"

"No, he wasn't."

"How about those boys at the Bullshead this morning?"

Jeff's eyes narrowed. "You stay away from them, too. They're hardcases if ever I saw one, and I've seen plenty in my time."

"Ira said Nolan was talking to them last night."

"There's no law against talking to men in a saloon." Jeff leaned forward, jaw thrust stubbornly forward. "Dammit, Ethan, stay out of it. I'll take care of looking for your pa's killer."

"Does that mean you don't think Ben did it?"

"It means," Jeff said testily, "that I'm still investigating the case. Or will be when people quit pestering me with questions I don't have answers for."

Remembering what Joel had told him, Ethan said: "Did you know Nate Kestler's been seeing Tom Handleman's daughter?"

"Uhn-huh, I did. Your brother's got a big mouth when he's drunk, and he was pretty tipsy when Lou herded him in here yesterday." Jeff stood and tugged at his gun belt as if he wished he could take it off. "Go on back to the Bar-Five, Ethan. You being here is only going to cause more trouble."

"I think I'll hang and rattle a while, Jeff. You might need some help later on."

"Don't even think about that. The more distance you keep between yourself and the rest of the factions in town today, the less my chances of having to haul your carcass over to Manson's."

Ethan shrugged and buckled on his belt. He had no intention of leaving Sundance today. They both knew that. He paused when he reached the door, glanced back a final time at the map on the wall above Jeff's desk, all the little cañons where so many of his friends were either dying or disappearing. Something about the map was tugging at him, but he couldn't see it. Not yet, anyway.

Pulling open the door, Ethan walked outside just as Ralph Finch stepped onto the boardwalk, a cloth-covered tray balanced on one arm. He stopped when he saw Ethan, his gaze dropping guiltily to the steaming cloth, then up again, defiantly.

Stepping close to the deputy, Ethan smiled and said: "If Jeff catches you spitting in that food, he'll make you eat it. If I catch you doing it, I'll bust out every damn' tooth in your mouth."

Finch's face turned deep red, but he didn't reply. He slipped past Ethan and ducked inside, heeling the door shut behind him with a bang.

Chapter Ten

Leaving the sheriff's office, Ethan returned to Carver's snug little home on the edge of town.

Claudia met him at the door, ushered him inside with a finger to her lips. "The doctor is sleeping," she whispered.

Nodding acknowledgment, Ethan asked softly: "How's Vic?"

"The same, which gives us hope."

It wasn't much, Ethan reflected, yet he felt more relief than he would have expected at her words. Vic was still alive. He'd half anticipated a different answer.

"If you'd like to see him, you may, although the doctor prefers that he not be disturbed."

"Then I won't," Ethan said. "I'll come back later to check on him."

"Have you eaten?" she asked.

"I had some breakfast at the Occidental, and I'm not hungry. I expect I'd better go talk to Roy Manson now. I need to ask him about burying Pa, since I don't figure I'll get back to the Bar-Five anytime soon." He touched the brim of his hat. "Thank you for everything, ma'am."

Claudia pursed her lips in reproach. "How many times must I ask you to address me by my given name, Mister Wilder?"

"I'll work on that . . . Claudia."

The woman smiled, gray eyes twinkling with amusement. "Now, that wasn't so hard, was it, Ethan?"

"No, ma'am, it wasn't," he replied, stepping through the door. "I'll be back later to see Vic."

Most of Sundance's business district was stretched out along Hide Street, but a few smaller shops ran west down Culver. Roy Manson's Cabinet Shop and Mortuary was one of them, a narrow building of ship-lapped lumber half a block down from the sheriff's office. A thumb-sized bell over the door tinkled pleasantly as Ethan entered a nearly empty front room smelling strongly of freshly planed wood and varnish. There was a dusty desk in one corner, a file cabinet beside it; a full-length curtain in the rear wall shielded the rest of the building from outside curiosity. Ethan had barely closed the door when Manson pushed through the curtain, a stocky man of middling age, curly gray hair, bald on top. His expression sobered professionally when he recognized Ethan.

"I've been expecting you, Mister Wilder," Roy said. "I assume you've come to make arrangements for your father?"

"I have."

"Doctor Carver asked me to prepare the deceased yesterday. I hope that wasn't presumptuous?"

Ethan shrugged, feeling suddenly as awkward as he had the first time he'd viewed his pa's body, back in Doc's office. "Where is he?" he asked.

"This way." Roy held the curtain aside.

Ethan stepped into a large back room. To the left, a corner had been set apart with ornate curtains hanging from the wall, an Oriental rug on the floor. There was a small table with a potted plant, its leaves curled and brown, and a settee upholstered in red and beige paisley. A simple, cherry-stained pine coffin sat on a wooden platform in front of the settee, while an overhead lamp cast forgiving light over the somber nook. Ethan's puzzled glance took in the rest of the room—a standard carpenter's shop, carpeted in wood shavings.

"Very few people hold their wakes here," Roy explained apologetically. "Most feel the home is more appropriate."

"I expect it is under normal circumstances," Ethan agreed.

"Would you like to view the deceased?"

"Naw, I can see just fine from here." In afterthought, Ethan removed his hat. "Where'd he get his clothes?"

"Doctor Carver authorized a new set of work clothing to be billed to his account," Roy said. "In appreciation of all your father did for Sundance."

"You mean when the whole damn' town nearly starved and froze to death that first winter?" Ethan asked, the words tumbling out harsher than he meant for them to.

Stoically Roy replied: "I assume. I wasn't here then."

Ethan sighed and brought his feelings back under control. "What do we do now?"

"We can do whatever you wish . . . although, with the unusual heat we've been experiencing recently, I'd suggest a quick decision."

"Can we bury him in the Sundance cemetery until things slow down?"

"Of course. Do you need to purchase a plot?"

"Roy, I don't know what the hell I need. Just tell me what it'll cost to put my old man underground, those new clothes included, and when you'll have him ready."

Roy's expression softened. "I'm not sure how much Doc spent on the clothes, but they don't look expensive. Total costs for a simple service, including coffin and wooden headboard, is twelve dollars. Figure another three to have the grave dug, then covered again, will bring the total to fifteen dollars. I'm afraid you'll have to take up the cost of the clothes with Doctor Carver." He hesitated as if embarrassed. "Normally I'd wait until after the services to present a bill, but . . ."

"But I might not be around long enough afterward to pay?"

"I have a wife and children, Ethan. I have to feed them."

Ethan dug a handful of coins, most of them double eagles, from his poke and tossed them, one at a time, across the room.

Roy caught them deftly with one hand, then switched them to his other hand just as smoothly to snag the next coin out of the air. His eyes widened when the saw the amount.

"That's for Pa and me and Vic and any other Wilder that doesn't come through the next few days alive. You figure that'll cover five funerals?"

His embarrassment deepening, Roy dropped the coins into the pocket of his canvas carpenter's apron. "You can pick up your change anytime."

Ethan inclined his head toward his father's body. "How long?"

"I'll need to fasten the lid on the coffin, then hitch a team. I store the hearse in one of Tim Palmer's sheds. It'll be covered with dust . . ."

"A little dust never hurt anyone," Ethan interrupted, feeling a need to get this done as soon as possible and move on. "I'll be back in an hour." He spun on his heels and stalked through the heavy curtain to the front office.

Roy Manson's voice trailed after him like a cringing pup. "I'm sorry for your loss, Ethan. Your father was a good . . ."

Ethan slammed the front door shut behind him, whatever else Roy had intended to say about Jacob Wilder lost in the bang.

* * * * *

Ethan stood on the boardwalk in front of Manson's and took a deep breath. The rush of emotions that had nearly over-whelmed him inside the mortuary began to lessen in the warm, early afternoon sun. Standing there, staring south past empty, weed-choked lots, he suddenly realized he could see Lou Mer-rick's house over on Cemetery Street. On impulse, he crossed in that direction.

The Merricks lived in a small, square building with a peaked roof and tiny porch out front. There was a barn in back, although Ethan knew Lou didn't own a horse. In spite

of Merrick's reputation as the town's handyman, both structures looked in bad shape. The roof was peeling at the eaves
and the molding had come off above one of the windows on
the house, leaving a slot large enough for a man to slip his hand
through. If the house had ever been any other color than the
wind-scoured and paintless gray it was today, Ethan couldn't see
any evidence of it.

Standing at the corner of a coal shed on the north side of
Cemetery Street, Ethan studied the house for several minutes.
He didn't really know Merrick, wasn't even sure if they'd ever
spoken to one another, but his opinion of the man had never
been very high. Lou Merrick was no stranger to the bottle, and
was known to turn foul-mouthed and belligerent when drunk.
He was considered lazy by most standards, although it was said
that, when he was sober, he could hammer a hundred nails
without bending one, and saw through oak in half the time it
took another man.

As Ethan watched, an out-of-sight door screeched open on
loose hinges. Moments later, Lou's wife—he didn't even know
her name—appeared, heading for the barn with a woven egg
basket hooked over one arm. Ethan waited until she'd disappeared inside, then crossed the street to the front porch. Lou
must have seen him coming, because Ethan hadn't even knocked
when the door was yanked open and Lou stepped outside with a
Whitney-Kennedy rifle leveled at Ethan's belt buckle.

"Stay back, Wilder," Merrick ordered sharply.

"Easy, boss," Ethan said quickly, raising both hands part way.
"I just came to talk."

"Ain't you Wilders done enough damage around here?"

"That's what I'm trying to find out," Ethan said.

"There ain't nothing more to find out," Merrick snarled.
"That crazy brother of yours tried to have his way with my little
girl. When he saw he couldn't get it, he beat the hell out of her."

"That's not the story I heard," Ethan replied calmly.

"Yeah, from who? Your brother?" Merrick laughed, then spat off the porch.

Anger had been a constant companion of Ethan's ever since returning to Sundance; it surged now, spilling over into his eyes.

Merrick saw it and took a step back, jabbing his elbow into the door frame. He howled and his arm jerked, and Ethan snatched the Whitney-Kennedy from his grasp.

"Jesus," Merrick breathed, face going pale.

Ethan worked the lever rapidly, emptying the magazine, then tossed the rifle into the weeds beside the house. "I ought to bend that barrel over your damn' head," he said hotly.

"If I hadn't hit my funny bone, you wouldn't have taken it away from me. We'd've seen then how tough you were."

"I'll tell you what, Lou," Ethan said so quietly Merrick unconsciously leaned forward to hear him better. "It's even now, just you and me, so let's see how tough I am."

Merrick shook his head. "I ain't fightin' you, Wilder. That'd just give you an excuse to stick a knife in me, or shoot me when my back was turned."

Ethan's eyes blazed. "You may not like us, Merrick, but I'll guarantee you that, if any Wilder ever decides to shoot you, it won't be in the back, and it won't be when you're unarmed."

"You Wilders ain't nothing but Indian lovers and horse thieves," Merrick said, but he was shrinking back as he said it, raising an arm defensively.

Ethan's fist clenched. He wanted to slam it into Merrick's face, smash the hateful leer into the flooring. Then someone came around the corner of the house and Ethan shook his head as if coming out of a deep sleep.

Merrick's wife stopped when she saw Ethan towering over her husband, cupping both hands over her mouth as if to stifle a scream. Her obvious terror triggered quick embarrassment in Ethan, and he stepped back, then plunged off the porch.

"You gonna run now, Wilder?" Lou shouted after him. "Afraid of having a witness to your trickery?"

Ethan kept walking. It galled him that he'd nearly allowed Merrick's words to goad him into doing something stupid, risking not only his own freedom, but perhaps the lives of Ben and Joel. He would have to watch himself, he realized, keep a lid on his temper, else he would play right into the hands of the unknown element trying so hard to have him, to have all the Wilders, removed from the territory.

Chapter Eleven

It was midafternoon when they laid Jacob Wilder to rest in the Sundance Cemetery, on the knoll southwest of town. Besides Ethan, there was Roy Manson, a couple of maintenance men with shovels standing well back from the service, and Claudia Carver, who had driven up in her buggy.

Had there been more time to get the word out, Ethan figured there would have been a larger crowd, but he had to wonder just how much larger. Ira Webb surely would have come if not for the unusual number of customers who seemed to have taken up residence in the Bullshead recently, but Ethan wasn't as certain about men like Sam Davidson and Tim Palmer and their families. Would they have closed their shops for an hour or so to pay respects to a man whose generosity that first harsh winter had kept them alive? Or would they have shunned the funeral in favor of the current attitude, that the old-timers—the hunters and traders who had come West while the land was still raw and wild—were an embarrassment to the senses of a modern civilization spreading swiftly, irreversibly, across the continent?

The last few days had been eye-opening ones for Ethan, who'd gradually come to realize that the animosity he was receiving from the townspeople had actually been there for a long time, a festering wound finally scratched open by Joel's alleged mistreatment of Suzie Merrick, and the charge that it had been Ben who'd killed Jacob. Standing at the foot of his father's grave, listening to Roy Manson read from the Bible, Ethan felt an incredible sadness creep over him, a feeling of isolation and vulnerability. Then he heard his name spoken, and looked up to find Roy watching him, Bible closed.

"Would you like to toss in the first handful of earth, Ethan?"

Nodding dutifully, Ethan picked up a handful of soil that he tossed in on top of Jacob's flat-topped coffin, the rattle of dirt on wood like shot peppering his soul.

Claudia Carver came over afterward to lay a hand on his arm. "I'm so sorry, Ethan. For your loss here, and for Victor and the troubles that plague Joel and Ben. Mister Carver would have come, if not for the need to stay at your brother's side. He asked me to extend his condolences, and to invite you to supper tonight. You will come, won't you?"

Ethan took a deep breath, expelled it shakily. "Yes, ma'am, I'd be honored."

"We'll eat at six, but come early. Victor is showing signs of improvement. I know he'd like to see you if he regains consciousness."

"Is he getting better?" Ethan asked, then wished he hadn't when he saw the look on her face.

"We can only pray that he does," Claudia said. She gave his arm a friendly squeeze. "I'd best get back, but know that we're keeping you in our prayers, Ethan. All of you."

"Thank you. I reckon I could use all the help I can get." He walked her to the buggy and helped her inside, then freed the tether weight from the horse's bit and dropped it on the floorboard.

"I'll see you at six, if not before," he promised.

Ethan had ridden up Cemetery Hill on the hearse with Roy Manson, but he declined a lift back into town, preferring some time alone to sort through his thoughts. Everything had been happening so fast lately that he was beginning to feel like a drunk on a runaway horse, barely hanging onto his hat.

The road was dusty, the sun warm on his back. Meadowlarks skimmed along in the grass beside him, singing their warning of a stranger in their midst. Like the meadowlarks, Ethan's mind flitted rapidly. What was going on, not just with his own family, but with the whole region? So many men missing or murdered in the breaks, yet hardly a mention of it up here. And what did they have, those woolly, unwashed sons of the frontier, that was worth killing for? Land might have been a common factor, and easy enough to understand with the Bar-Five's homesteaded water holes, but old Emile Rodale and Ian McMillan had never filed a claim in their lives. And why would someone want to hang Ian's woman, who couldn't have claimed the land even if she'd wanted to, being Blackfoot.

What else made sense? Water? There was the whole of the Marias for that. Gold? Ethan had never heard of any precious metals being found this far out on the plains; gold was a mountain commodity, a lure of the high country. Grass? Except for the Bar-Five—which had never exercised its rights anyway—there was no impediment to running cattle on the open range anywhere along the Marias, and certainly none that would require the systematic extermination of a bunch of ex-hunters and their Indian and mixed-blood families.

It has to be something else, Ethan thought. *It has to.*

His gaze strayed to Palmer's Livery, and his pace slowed. He knew there were people around town who rented out extra stable space to local residents who didn't have their own facilities, but only Tim Palmer made a business of it. He owned the livery, ran a blacksmith shop, and bought and sold hay on the side. Seen from the rear as he hiked down from Cemetery Hill, Ethan was struck by the size of Palmer's sprawling complex of barn, sheds, and corrals. He hadn't realized it was so extensive, taking up several acres behind the red-painted, street-front entrance of his main stables. A man could board a horse overnight in that big barn if he wanted to have it fed and watered, even curried. But if he planned on staying long, or had several head to care for, most men would rent one of the corrals out back.

Abruptly Ethan veered off the road to follow a wagon lane into the heart of holding pens and corrals. As he made his way down the central aisle, he occasionally allowed the inside of his forearm to brush the butt of his revolver. There was no reason to expect trouble, yet he felt unaccountably nervous, his throat dry and scratchy.

Rough count, Ethan estimated sixty-plus head of livestock scattered throughout the pens. The largest corral was occupied by mules carrying the Diamond T Freight company's brand, but he recognized several animals belonging to some of Sundance's wealthier citizens—Sam Davidson's tall bay and Ray Manson's sorrel among them. Others carried local brands, including a trio of cow ponies sporting Kestler's Lazy-K. It was in one of the smaller corrals close to the main stables that Ethan finally found what he was looking for—eight head of quality horses, all with unfamiliar and unmatching brands.

Ethan's brows furrowed in thought. There had been six men sitting in back of the Bullshead that morning, including the one with a recently bloodied cheek. He was certain he'd killed one of the ambushers in the shallow creek behind the house yesterday, then wounded a second one minutes later, probably the man Doc Carver had treated. He was also pretty sure he'd drawn blood on a third man, too, judging from the shrill cursing from the barn after firing several rounds at the empty water barrel in the entryway. That brought him back to the Bullshead, and the man with the torn cheek.

Eight horses . . . eight men.

Ethan's pulse quickened as he entered a side door to Palmer's Livery. He came to a wide entryway, cool and dim. He saw no one, but heard movement in the office near the front door, and headed in that direction.

Tim Palmer looked up from his desk when Ethan entered the cramped room, an alarmed expression coming over his face. He pushed his chair back even as he yanked open a top drawer.

Catching a glimpse of a nickel-plated pocket revolver inside, Ethan instinctively kicked the drawer closed, barely avoiding smashing Palmer's fingers. The liveryman jumped to his feet, cursing, and tried to back away, but Ethan grabbed a fistful of shirt and jerked him close.

"What's the matter, Timmy? Has something got you spooked?"

"Let go of me, Wilder."

"Not until you tell me what happened to the missing man who rode in here yesterday?"

"I don't know what you're talking about."

"I think you do." He pulled the drawer open and grabbed the revolver. "You wouldn't think you needed this if you didn't." He tossed the small handgun behind the desk. "You've got eight horses out there with brands I've never seen before. Where are the men who ride them?" Palmer clamped his mouth shut, and Ethan gave him a quick but violent shake. "Don't take that trail, Timmy. I don't have the patience for it today."

"All right!" Palmer cried, throwing his hands up in surrender. "I don't know where they are . . ."

"I told you I don't . . ."

"Wait, dammit, I'll tell you." He took a deep breath. "Let me go first."

Ethan released his grip, giving the hostler a little backward shove to keep him off balance. "All right, talk."

"Geez, Ethan, are you insane? You can't just come in here . . ."

"I warned you about wasting my time."

"You can't come in here and treat me like this in my own business. I've got rights in this town."

Ethan moved forward. Palmer tried to dodge out of reach, but he was too slow. Catching the liveryman's collar and taking a firm hold on the seat of his trousers, Ethan threw him out the door.

Palmer slammed into the stall across the aisle, then stumbled back, blood smeared across his upper lip. There was a pitchfork leaning against the wall beside him and he grabbed it, but Ethan had already picked up a twitch—made from an axe handle, used to calm unruly horses during shoeing or doctoring—and batted the pitchfork out of Palmer's hands. Palmer stumbled backward, tripped over his own feet, and fell with an explosive grunt. Ethan stood over him, the solid oak twitch ready to swing again.

"I'll tell you what," he said dangerously. "You tell me what I want to know, then you can run over and complain to Jeff Burke about what a mean son-of-a-bitch I am."

"This isn't right," Palmer mumbled indignantly. "I would've told you what you wanted to know. All you had to do was ask."

"You're going to tell me this way, too, and I'll get a straight answer without a lot of smug opinions."

Palmer's lips thinned at the injustice of his predicament, but he didn't argue further. "I don't know who they are. They pay their bill, I take care of their horses."

"You know the name of the man who pays you?"

Palmer hesitated, then shrugged. "Fact is, Nolan Andrews pays their bill."

No surprise there, Ethan thought grimly. "What's Andrews's connection to them?"

"You'd have to ask them that," Palmer replied. "In case you haven't noticed, they aren't a talkative bunch."

Ethan lowered the twitch. "There are eight horses out there. Where is Andrews's mount?"

"Andrews keeps his horse stabled inside."

"There were only six men in the Bullshead this morning. Where are the other two?"

"It isn't my job to keep track of customers," Palmer replied testily. After a pause, he added: "If you let me get up, I'll show you something."

Ethan stepped back, tossed the twitch into the office. "Show me."

Palmer led him to the large tack room behind the office. "Andrews's men have those saddle racks near the back," he said, pointing. "Take a look at those two farthest saddles."

Ethan gave Palmer a measured glance. "Don't wander off, Timmy."

"I'm not going anywhere."

Ethan went over to the saddles. It didn't take long to spot what had caught the hostler's eyes. Both hulks were tracked with rust-colored stains over the horns and pommels, and Ethan's eyes narrowed in recognition. "Blood," he murmured, and turned just in time to see the heel of a scoop shovel descending from above.

Chapter Twelve

There was an ache in his neck and shoulders, and the back of his head throbbed painfully. Opening his eyes, Ethan squinted at his surroundings. He knew where he was almost immediately, and turned his head toward the door, wincing at the quick stabbing in his skull. Jeff Burke stood in the opening, leaned wearily against its frame.

"Just like old times, huh, Ethan?" Jeff asked without humor.

"Not quite," Ethan replied gruffly. He swung his legs carefully off the bunk and sat up.

"What happened?"

"Palmer says you got feisty and he had to cold cock you."

"Oh, yeah." Ethan chuckled. "Is that what he said?"

Jeff shrugged without interest. "Palmer and one of his hired men toted you over. Palmer wanted to press charges, but I told him I'd have to think about it."

Ethan didn't try to deny any wrongdoing on his part, having never developed the habit of lying to excuse his actions. The fact was, he'd lost his temper when Palmer reached for the gun in his drawer, and that was the long and short of it right there. "You made up your mind yet?" he asked.

"I ought to keep you locked up. It would make my job simpler. I hear you paid Lou Merrick a visit, too, and scared his wife half out of her mind. Is that true?"

"I was there. I couldn't say about Missus Merrick. Did anyone mention he had a rifle pointed at my belly?"

"He didn't mention a rifle."

"I'd wager there's a lot of things Lou Merrick ain't mentioned," Joel said from the next cell. "Especially about me 'n' that girl of his."

"Shut up, Joel," Jeff said mildly. He studied Ethan quietly for another minute, then sighed and straightened. "I need some more time to think about those charges. Until I make up my mind, you get out of here. Just don't go back to Merrick's or Palmer's, savvy?"

"I savvy."

"Shy clear of the Bullshead, too."

Ethan stood, exited the cell on wobbly legs.

"Ethan!" Joel hissed, pressing tightly against the flat straps of iron holding him prisoner. "Get us outta here. Burke's gonna run when Kestler comes in, and that son-of-a-bitch and his cowboys are gonna hang me 'n' Ben for sure."

"I'm not going to tell you again to shut your trap," Jeff growled. "Another word out of you and I'll come in there and put a gag on you."

"Stay out of trouble," Ethan told his brothers, then followed the sheriff into the front room. His hat and gun belt were sitting on the desk. He strapped the belt around his waist, but held off putting on his hat. "Did Palmer tell you about the blood on those saddles, or that Nolan Andrews has been paying the stable bill for those hardcases over at the Bullshead?"

"He mentioned it. As long as the bill gets paid, it's none of my business who shells out the money, and getting blood on saddle leather is hardly new."

"Those men work for Andrews, Jeff. That's got to mean something."

Burke flopped into his chair. "I'll tell you the truth, Ethan . . . right now I'm too damn' tired to even jump to a conclusion about what Nolan Andrews and those boys over at the Bullshead are up to, let alone walk over there to find out."

"Then what are you going to do?"

"I'm going to sit here and wait for Charlie Kestler to come in. Then I'm going to try like hell to keep a lid on his temper, because the word is, Charlie's bringing a couple of strong ropes with him. When I've got that situation under control, and had a few hours sleep in my own bed, I'll start looking at those bloody saddles and maybe ask Andrews what he knows about them. But right now, I'm staying put."

The impatience that had been growing against the sheriff disappeared. "I reckon that makes sense," Ethan conceded.

"I'm glad you approve," Jeff replied cynically. "Now why don't you make my job easier and get out of town for a spell?"

"I'm not going anywhere until this is settled."

"Then go over to Doc Carver's and sit with Vic. And keep a halter on that temper of yours. It'll only make things worse if you don't."

Ethan didn't reply. His attention had been captured again by the map above the sheriff's desk. Mentally he traced the line of murders and disappearances in the breaks. For a moment, he thought he'd spotted something, but, when he looked closer, it was gone.

"Go on, Ethan," Jeff said gently. "Go look in on Vic. . . ."

The sheriff's words trailed off, and a funny look came to his face. In that same instant, Ethan became aware of a faint vibration through the soles of his boots.

"Son-of-a-bitch," Jeff said, standing and going to the door. As he pulled it open, a gust of fresh air swept into the room, bringing with it a faint rumble, like a stampede over the horizon. Without looking back, he said: "Get out of here, Wilder. Use the back door and stay out of sight."

"I can help."

"If you want to help, get out of here now." Jeff slammed the front door closed and bolted it, then went to the gun rack on the wall and lifted a double-barreled shotgun from it. Flashing Ethan a warning look, he added: "I mean it. If you aren't out of here by the time I get this scatter-gun loaded and closed, I'm going to throw you back in that empty cell beside your brothers and lock the door."

"All right, but I'll be close," Ethan said. He went out the back door, and Jeff locked it after him. In front, the sound of approaching horses grew steadily louder. Hurrying over to the high windows that allowed fresh air into the cells, Ethan called: "Joel, Ben, can you hear me?"

Fists appeared at both windows, knuckles tightening as the two prisoners hauled themselves up high enough to see out. "Ethan," Ben cried, "what's going on?"

Joel was more to the point. "God dammit, Eth, get us outta here."

"Listen, Kestler's here, and it sounds like he's got a full crew."

"It sounds like he's got an army," Joel said.

"Dammit, listen to me," Ethan said impatiently. "I've two horses in the barn behind Carver's house. If things get out of hand and I have to break you out of here, remember that. I'll make sure they're saddled and bridled. If you have to make a run for it, head for Elk Camp. I'll join you there as soon as I can."

"Things are already out of hand," Joel said desperately. "Get us outta here!"

"Not yet," Ethan replied. "Let's see what Jeff does before we dig ourselves in any deeper."

"Ethan," Ben said plaintively.

"Yeah, little Brother?"

"Ethan, I don't wanna die." Ben sounded close to tears, fear thrumming his voice like chords on a guitar.

Ethan's fists clenched in frustration. "Remember those horses, Ben. If you have to run, grab one and don't look back. I'll be close behind you."

* * * * *

Ethan kept to the alleys and back lots as he made his way around to Sam Davidson's Mercantile. He entered through the rear door, then followed a narrow aisle to the front of the store.

Davidson and his sallow-faced clerk were at the window, staring down the street toward the sheriff's office. There were no customers, and Sam's glare seemed to indicate he considered Ethan to be the cause.

"Hell's about to break loose now, Wilder," Sam said accusingly. "We'll be lucky if Kestler doesn't take a torch to this town."

"Kestler isn't interested in destroying Sundance," Ethan replied. "He wants Joel."

"And what do you think he'll do if he doesn't get him?"

"If he's the gentleman you seem to believe he is, he'll go home and wait until Burke finishes his investigation."

Sam snorted derisively. "Charlie Kestler is a lot of things, but I don't know anyone who'd consider him a gentleman. You don't build a ranch the size of the Lazy-K by waiting for someone else to do your dirty work. Kestler wants Joel, and he'll raise holy hell until he gets him, including turning his cowboys loose on the town."

Ethan stared out the window to where Kestler had halted his crew in front of the sheriff's office. He was startled by the size of the rancher's command. The last he'd heard, Kestler ran a small but growing spread northwest of Sundance, supplying beef to the Blackfoot Reservation and the Army at Fort Shaw. He'd had only three or four men working for him then, including his son Nate.

There were at least twenty men sitting, tight-reined and flint-eyed, behind the rancher today. Nate was there, mounted on a flashy palomino at his father's side, taller and slimmer than Ethan remembered him, a revolver on each hip.

"When did Charlie Kestler get so big?" Ethan asked.

"Working from dawn until after dark, while you Wilders were chasing squaws down in the breaks," Sam replied curtly. Ethan turned slowly, and Davidson gulped and took a step back. "I, ah . . . I didn't mean it to sound like that, Ethan. I just meant to say Kestler's been working hard, bringing in fresh stock from Oregon to build up his herd, things like that."

"I used to consider you a friend," Ethan said softly. "That's why I'm not going to break your jaw right now. But if you ever say anything like that again, I will. Not your arm or a rib, but your jaw, so you can think about that big mouth of yours while sipping soup for a couple of months. Do you believe me, Sam?"

The shopkeeper's face had faded to the color of quartz. "Yeah, I believe you," he croaked.

Ethan glanced at Davidson's clerk, standing motionlessly behind his boss. Becoming aware of a faintly acidic stink, Ethan glanced at the clerk's trousers. A dark stain had appeared under the fly, spreading slowly. Wrinkling his nose, Ethan said: "Go home, and keep your head down. Things are going to get ugly around here real soon."

* * * * *

Kestler reined up in front of the sheriff's office, his men coming to a rough stop behind him. The fine dust from the street swirled forward, enveloping the horsemen in a powdery fog. No one spoke until it settled. Then the jailhouse door swung open and Jeff Burke stepped onto the boardwalk. He carried his shotgun muzzles down in his right hand, his left hooked by the thumb to his gun belt. His voice carried faintly to those waiting and watching in Davidson's store.

"You're wasting your time, Mister Kestler. I'm not going to turn Joel Wilder over to you or anyone else."

"I didn't come here just for Joel Wilder, Jeff. I came to bring justice to this land. I want 'em both."

"Bastard," Ethan mouthed.

"They'll stand trial for their crimes, and, if they're found guilty, they'll be punished in accordance with the law."

"A jury of their peers?" Kestler asked.

"That's right."

"And who is that?"

"Men from the community."

"Men like these?" Kestler tipped his head toward the cowboys behind him.

"No, sir. Men who are court appointed, who live and work in Sundance, and have a vested interest in seeing law prevail over revenge. All you have here is a mob."

"It took a mob to clean up Ruby Gulch." Kestler's voice rose dramatically. "A mob of citizens willing to do what a bunch of timid lawmen were either powerless to do, or too damn' faint-hearted."

"Those days are over," Jeff replied firmly. "We have an established law now, and a judicial system to see that it's carried out properly. I won't tolerate vigilantism in Sundance. Go home, Charlie. Let me handle this."

Kestler leaned forward in his saddle, reminding Ethan of a vulture readying itself for flight. His men waited expectantly, hands hovering near their guns. For one agonizing moment, Ethan thought Kestler was going to give the command to swarm the jail. Then, just as suddenly, the rancher leaned back, seemingly growing smaller before Ethan's eyes. But he wasn't cowed. Even from Davidson's, Ethan could tell he hadn't given up.

"We'll talk later, Jeff," Kestler said, raising his voice once more for the benefit of those who watched from behind closed doors. "After my boys have had a couple of drinks."

Jeff's shoulders twitched at the implication. "Keep your men sober, Kestler. I don't want a bunch of drunken cowboys shooting up the town."

Ethan felt Davidson's eyes shift toward him, as if to say I told you so. Ethan didn't return the look.

Kestler jerked his horse around and trotted it down the street to the Bullshead. His men came after him, filling the hitching rails on either side of the saloon. Jeff remained on the boardwalk another minute, then went inside.

When he was gone, Ethan made his way to the back door. He half expected some scathing remark from Davidson, but only the echo of his own boots accompanied him outside.

He took the back way to Carver's, staying out of sight of anyone lingering along the main thoroughfare, and knocked softly on the window glass to Doc's office.

The physician opened the door. Eyeing Ethan's bare head, he said: "You've got straw in your hair, Ethan."

"I've got a lump up there, too."

"You Wilders have been good for business lately. I wish you'd quit it. Let me have a look."

"Kestler's in town."

"You think I don't know that? Sit down."

Ethan hung his hat on a rack made of antelope horns, then folded himself wearily into a chair.

Doc probed gently at the hardened knot at the back of Ethan's skull, then wiped his hands on a towel. "I'm assuming you were poking your nose where it didn't belong."

"Depends on your point of view."

"Well, I don't know if you'll live or not, but it won't be that bump on your head that kills you."

"How's Vic?"

Carver's expression relaxed in a faint smile. "He's been awake off and on. Would you like to see him?"

"I would." Ethan pushed to his feet and followed Carver into the small room off of his office. Vic was lying on his back, blankets folded down to his waist. He looked pale and wasted, and Ethan's smile dimmed. "Hey, little Brother, how are you feeling?" he asked gently.

Vic's gaze shifted listlessly toward the sound of his voice. His eyes were dull and pain-filled, but at least they were open.

"Can you hear me?" Ethan asked.

After a pause, Vic's head moved in a small nod. He didn't try to speak.

Leaning close, Ethan said: "Vic, I need to know. Did you see the man who shot you?"

There was another long silence, followed by a faint scowl and a barely perceptible nod. Then Vic's eyes rolled back in his head and Ethan's heart felt like it had stopped beating until he noticed the steady rise and fall of his brother's shrunken torso.

"Jesus," Ethan gasped.

"He's sleeping," Doc said. "That'll do him more good than anything I can give him. Let's let him rest."

"I need to know who shot him, Doc. For Ben's sake."

"I know, but it'll have to wait."

Ethan nodded, eyes blurring as he followed Carver back to his office. He knew that, with Kestler in town, time was running out. Despite his vow to Joel and Ben to break them out if he had to, he knew pulling off a jailbreak would be next to impossible. There had to be another way.

"Doc, you said Vic was shot with a small-caliber gun?"

"In my opinion, yes. Of course, I haven't seen the bullet."

"Pa was shot with a small caliber, too. Could it have been the same gun?"

"It's not only possible, I made note of it in the sheriff's report I filled out on Vic."

"What caliber?"

"I still have the bullet I dug out of your father, if you'd like to see it." Doc was already moving toward the big roll-top desk against the wall.

Ethan followed, his expression wooden as the physician dropped a lead slug into his palm.

"About a Thirty-Two," he heard himself say above the roaring in his ears. And deep in his mind, Ben's voice: *Pa bought himself a neat little rifle, a Thirty-Two pump, and he caught me using it to shoot flies off the ceiling in the kitchen.*

This had all started because of that little .32 pump-action rifle, Ethan reflected, *but where was it now?* He hadn't seen it when he and Vic were straightening up the house. He rolled the half-flattened slug under his thumb.

"It killed Pa, but it didn't kill Vic," he pondered aloud.

"That's because your father was shot at pointblank range," Doc said. "Vic was shot from farther away."

"Yeah, from the barn."

"What are you driving at?"

Ethan shook his head. "I don't know. Do you mind if I keep this?"

"Not at all."

"Thanks." Ethan dropped the bullet in his pocket, lifted his hat from the wall rack, then hesitantly put it back. "Would you mind if I stayed here a while?"

"I'd consider it a wise decision," Doc replied solemnly. "Claudia is preparing supper. She mentioned she invited you to share it with us."

Ethan nodded. "If that's all right."

Doc smiled and grasped his shoulder with affection. "Of course it is, and about time we repaid a fraction of our debt to the Wilders."

"You don't owe us anything, Doc, especially after what you've done for Vic. I'm obliged for that." Moving toward the back door, he said: "I'll check on the horses if there's time."

"Plenty of time. Supper won't be ready for another couple of hours."

Ethan paused with his hand on the knob. "If Vic wakes up and I'm not here, ask him to describe the man who shot him, would you?"

For a moment, Doc looked like he was going to refuse. Then his features softened. "I won't do anything that might cause him discomfort, but . . . if I can, I will."

Ethan nodded his thanks and exited the office. In Doc's barn, he found the Appaloosa and sorrel still tied off in separate stalls, hay and fresh water within easy reach. Pulling a currycomb from a box nailed to the wall, he began working on the Appaloosa's rust-spotted coat. The horse was just green-broke, skittish at the unfamiliar sensations of the brush, but Ethan took his time, enjoying the simplicity of the chore, the calming effect it had on him as much as the horse. On just the ride in from the Bar-Five, he'd already grown fond of the animal. It was easily the equal of his bay, and better than any of the other horses in his personal string. If things worked out—meaning he didn't end up dead in the next few hours or days—he wanted to put more work in with the Appaloosa, train it gently.

He curried the sorrel next, then saddled and bridled both horses, drawing the cinches tight because he knew that, if Joel and Ben needed mounts, they would need them in a hurry.

Leaving the horses in the barn, Ethan took his rifle and shell belt and went around the front of the house to the small porch. The wicker chair where he'd slept last night sat to the left of the door, catching the full rays of the afternoon sun, but a couple of comfortable-looking rockers set back in the shade of trellises woven through with green ivy caught his eye, and he settled gratefully into one of these. He dropped the heavy cartridge belt in a heap on the floor beside him, then laid the Winchester across his lap. Leaning back, he propped his heels on the porch railing and tried to relax.

From the Carvers' front porch, Sundance looked almost serene. Bees buzzed in the flower bed alongside the house, and hummingbirds darted back and forth like tiny gossips, blurred wings humming. Ethan could have slept if he'd allowed himself to, but he was afraid to let go. From here, he could see the jail, a couple of blocks down and across the street. The Bullshead was hidden from view, but in his mind's eye he could still see the line of horses strung out along the hitch rails, the hard faces of the men who'd ridden them into town.

Forcing his gaze away, toward the broad expanse of empty plains rolling in gentle swells to the south, Ethan spied a thin plume of dust rising into the sky. His eyes narrowed and his fingers slid unconsciously back over the Winchester's side plate to the rifle's steel lever. He slid three of them inside, ready to cock the piece for firing, forefinger curved toward the trigger.

Time crept past at an arthritic gait. The dust rose higher, but didn't thicken as it might have under a group of fast-approaching horsemen. Ethan took that as a good sign. After a bit, he stood and walked to the edge of the porch. It was a wagon rolling toward Sundance, its features vaguely familiar. As it drew nearer, he suddenly placed it, and said, under his breath: "You damn' old fool."

It took another thirty minutes for the outfit to reach town. As it drew even with the Carver house, Ethan almost stepped into the street to intercept it. Yet something stopped him, kept him rooted where he was as Gerard Turcotte guided his ancient rig down the middle of Hide Street.

Corn Grower sat on Gerard's right, Rachel on his left. All three glanced at him as they rattled past, but none offered even a gesture of recognition. When the wagon had rolled past, Ethan glanced south again. Trailing Turcotte's rig by half a mile was a second wagon. From its faded red canvas cover, Ethan recognized Badger Dick Barlow's trade wagon. The burly, apple-shaped figure of the gray-bearded old peddler and his Piegan wife sat side-by-side atop the tall seat, their full-grown sons riding alongside on scrawny Indian ponies, long-barreled rifles slanted across their saddlebows. They also passed without greeting, although Ethan knew they saw him. They followed after Turcotte, and, when they were hidden by Claudia Carver's rose bushes, Ethan looked south once more. Off in the distance, three more narrow columns of dust were spiraling into the sky, rolling in from the Marias' breaks like a storm front.

Chapter Thirteen

Supper at the Carvers' that night was roast beef, potatoes, carrots, and apple sauce. There was sweetened lemonade that Ethan ignored, coffee he drank black, and rice pudding for dessert. Under different circumstances, he would have considered it one of the best meals he'd ever eaten. As it was, he barely noticed the food passing his lips in the awkward silence that dominated the table.

By the time he was called in to eat, Ethan had watched no less than six hunter's wagons roll into town. They came in separately, as if by chance, but not one of them had acknowledged Ethan as they passed. Not even a nod. Something was up and Ethan was eager to know what it was, but instinct told him to proceed cautiously, that whatever was going on would reveal itself in time.

They were still seated at the table when they heard a staccato of pistol shots from the street. Ethan was out of his chair in a flash, grabbing his Winchester and shell belt on his way to the front door.

Following close behind, Doc lay a warning hand on the younger man's shoulder. "Don't go out there, son."

Ethan had no intention of rushing blindly outside. Leaning against the wall, he fingered a sheer out of his way to peer through the glass.

"What's happening?" Claudia asked fretfully from the dining room.

"Looks like some of Kestler's boys are blowing off steam," Ethan replied.

128

"Drunk, too, I'll wager," Doc said disapprovingly.

"Looks like it." Ethan watched a group of horsemen race their mounts down the street, whooping and hollering, firing their revolvers into the sky.

Doc's face grew taut with agitation. "This is Charlie Kestler's doing. He's deliberately trying to intimidate the town."

One glance at the doctor and his wife, and Ethan figured it wouldn't take much to do just that. "Kestler wouldn't risk the safety of innocent people," he argued. "He'll keep a rein on his boys."

"I'm afraid you don't know our Mister Kestler," Claudia replied.

"Now, we don't know if those rumors are true," Doc said, although without much conviction. He glanced at Ethan. "There have been stories that Kestler rode with Quantrill during the late war. To my knowledge, Kestler has never confirmed his role in the war . . ."

"Or denied it," Claudia interjected.

"Nor," Doc continued sternly, "have I ever heard anyone accuse him of any participation in the border wars."

"Those stories came from somewhere," Claudia replied stubbornly.

Ethan had been little more than a toddler when William Clarke Quantrill led his raiders into Lawrence, Kansas in one of the bloodiest attacks on civilians during the Civil War. Quantrill and his men had gone to Kansas seeking retribution for wrongs done to them and their families in Missouri, and they'd been in a vengeful mood the morning they overran Lawrence's skimpy guard. When they left town that afternoon, more than two hundred men and boys had been slaughtered, entire blocks ravaged by fire, women raped, homes and businesses plundered, wrecked. If Kestler did come from such a murderous background, Ethan figured that would change the rules significantly in regard to Joel and Ben. He spun away from the door, headed for Doc's office.

"Where are you going?" Doc asked.

"I want a closer look," Ethan flung back.

"Be careful!" Claudia called.

Ethan left the house and made his way past the barn, taking the back way to the Bullshead and staying out of sight as much as possible. The rear door to Ira Webb's living quarters was unlocked, and Ethan slipped inside, unnoticed. Nothing had changed since he'd awakened here the morning after his fight with Nolan Andrews—the single bunk was still unmade, same dirty laundry on the floor, dishes unwashed in the dry sink.

A closed door across the room led to a cluttered storage area, dimly lit by a single lantern. Beyond that was the main room and bar. Ethan eased past empty beer kegs and cases of sour mash to an inconspicuous door in the corner and cautiously eased it open a quarter of an inch. What he saw didn't look promising. There were at least twenty men—cowboys and merchants alike—lined up at the bar. Others stood around the big room drinking and talking, voices burred with anger. The men who had been there earlier—Nolan Andrews's men—were gone; Ethan would have given a $5 gold piece to know where they'd disappeared to.

Ira was handling the bar with hurried efficiency, keeping up with the demands for fresh drinks, but just barely. Right now the crowd seemed loud but contained, yet Ethan figured it wouldn't be long before things began to deteriorate.

It would start small, he reasoned, and probably be isolated within the saloon itself at first. A fist fight or smashed furniture, blood spilled, threats made. As the evening progressed, it would gradually spread outside. Cowboys would no longer be content to ride their horses in the street, and targets unnoticed before would suddenly present themselves—store windows, street lamps, maybe a passing citizen scrambling out of the way of bullets thrown at his heels. Eventually it would be as Davidson had predicted, the whole town engulfed in violence.

Unless someone stopped it.

That would be Kestler's job, but only if he wanted it. If he didn't, if he turned his back to it, dawn could well illuminate a town in ruin, Joel and Ben hanging from nooses as its centerpiece.

Ethan eased the door shut. He needed to get Ira back here, convince him to shut down the Bullshead. But how? Kestler's men were keeping him bumping, and Ethan knew he couldn't show his own face to those inside, already working themselves up for a lynching.

Glancing around the room, a case of empty whiskey bottles caught his eye. Leaning his rifle against the wall, Ethan picked it up and heaved it against the wall. The shattering glass made a lot more noise than he'd anticipated, and he quickly ducked behind the door in case someone other than Ira came to investigate.

In the front room, the rumble of conversation momentarily lessened, and Ethan slid his fingers around the Remington's worn grips. Then the racket picked up again, and the storage room door swung open. Ira stepped inside.

"What's goin' on in here?" the bartender shouted, a tautness to his voice Ethan had never heard before. When Ira stepped deeper into the room, Ethan kicked the door shut. Ira whirled, a leather blackjack raised. "Ethan!" he exclaimed. "Dammit, man, you scared the hell outta me."

"What are you doing out there?" Ethan demanded. "You know what's going to happen when those boys get drunk."

Ira lowered the lead-packed club. "Charlie Kestler's payin' me good money to keep the booze flowing. What can I do?"

"You can tell him you're going to close up, that no amount of money is worth what's going to happen when his men get so lacquered they can't be reasoned with."

"They're damn' near there now."

"Then put a stop to it!"

"I can't. Charlie gave me a hundred dollars to keep the Bullshead open, keep serving drinks till no one asks for more. He said, if the money ran out, I should start a tab and he'd pay me the rest later. Hell, Ethan, I can't turn my back on a hundred bucks."

"If you don't, you'll be turning your back on the whole town."

"Half the town's already in there. Sam Davidson, Tim Palmer, Lou Merrick. Even Ralph Finch is swillin' down drinks like he's never seen a whiskey glass before."

"Where are Andrews's men?"

"I couldn't say. They hightailed it soon as Kestler and his boys showed up."

Ethan shook his head and looked away. He felt helpless in the face of so many things spinning out of control, so many things that had never been in his control. "Ira, I'm asking you as a friend, shut this place down."

"I'd do it if I could, but that ain't no option no more. If I tried it now, them boys'd just take the place over." After a pause, he added: "I hate to say this, but you ought to go try to talk Jeff Burke into slippin' your brothers out the back way and hiding 'em somewhere, because, sooner or later, Kestler is gonna try to take 'em outta there by force."

Ethan doubted if Jeff would even listen to such an argument, let alone voluntarily release his two prisoners.

"I'm sorry, Ethan," Ira said softly, reaching for the door. "I truly am, but I gotta get back before some drunk cowboy takes a notion to climb over the bar and help hisself."

Ethan stared silently, at a loss for words, and Ira pulled the door open and slipped back into the main room. The raucous laughter momentarily grew louder, then faded again as the door swung shut. Ethan stood where he was for a moment, feeling the pulse of the crowd through the woodwork, then grabbed his rifle and wound back through the storeroom and outside.

The sun had set and the air was turning brisk. Ethan continued north through back alleys and empty lots, stopping at the edge of town. There was a dip in the land just outside of town, a low spot where the prairie grass was always a little lusher, a small spring at its head that ran the year around. It was where the hunters always made camp when they came to Sundance for supplies, and it was there that Ethan headed now, wanting to know what had brought so many old-timers into town at the same time.

Coming to the edge of the low bank, Ethan paused in surprise to see the hunters' wagons pulled up in a protective circle. It was something a man was more apt to see along the Overland Trail, or with a freight outfit going into camp for the night and needing a place to corral their mules or oxen. These men and women were a solitary breed, used to going their own way. As a rule, they avoided one another on the high plains, not out of animosity, but out of respect from another man's privacy. That they were huddled together now told Ethan a lot.

Gerard Turcotte's wagon was parked on the west side of the depression, and Ethan smiled when he saw Rachel bent over a small fire, stirring the contents of a cast-iron pot. He veered automatically in that direction, but hadn't gone more than a few paces when Badger Dick's two sons came out from behind their father's red-canvassed wagon and waved him over.

"Ethan!" the younger one called.

"Gabe," Ethan returned, then glanced at the older brother. "Howdy, Seth."

"Ethan," Seth returned, "Papa says you should come with us."

"Is there trouble?"

"Is there not always trouble of one kind or another?" Seth replied, smiling. "Come, Gerard also wishes to speak with you."

Ethan took a last, wistful look at the Turcotte camp, then turned away to follow Gabe and Seth to their father's Studebaker. He nodded a welcome to the men gathered there—Gerard and Badger Dick, Scotty Dunham, Hank McKay, François LaBarge. They returned his greeting warmly, these old friends of Jacob Wilder, most of whom could remember Ethan as a boy, just learning to ride and shoot.

"There is coffee," Badger Dick offered. "You would like a cup?"

"Coffee sounds good," Ethan concurred, shoulders hunching to the growing chill.

Kneeling next to the fire several yards away, Badger Dick's woman, Mary Many Robes, immediately dug a tin cup out of the parfleche container at her side. She filled it from a pot hanging over the low flames, and brought it to Ethan. He accepted gratefully, thanking her in his own awkward Piegan as she returned to her chores.

"You wonder why we come to Sundance, Ethan?" Gerard asked.

Ethan nodded. "I do, yes."

"We are here to seek justice from the white man's law."

Ethan eyed the old trader speculatively. "Since when has a hunter sought the laws of a foreign country for justice?"

The men grinned, murmured assent. They felt as Jacob had, that the citizens of Sundance were the interlopers, immigrants to a land they held no legal claim to. It obviously pleased them that Ethan shared their view.

Even solemn old Gerard smiled, but it was a short-lived display. Nodding toward Badger Dick's oldest son, he said: "Seth brought word three days ago that Tom Handleman was killed."

"Tom?" Ethan echoed, nearly choking on his coffee.

"I found his body in the Marias," Seth explained. "It had been there for several days."

"He was shot," Badger Dick added. "In the back."

"What about his wife and kids?"

"Swan's Wing and her children were not harmed, but Swan's Wing has already left to return to her people. Janey and the boys go with her."

Ethan's fingers tightened on his cup, the burn of the hot tin cool compared to the growing anger in his breast. "Who did it?" he asked.

"We don't know," Seth replied. "Swan's Wing says Tom was looking for buffalo in the breaks. She did not know he was dead until I brought her his body." After a pause, he added: "I buried him there, then helped Swan's Wing and Janey pack their belongings in a Red River cart and hitch up her horse. She left that night."

"And old Emile?" Ethan asked of Gerard.

"I have yet to find him, but I still believe I will." His voice became hard. "When this is settled."

"I've already talked to Jeff Burke about it," Ethan said. "He won't do anything until this business with Kestler is settled."

Squatting before a bare patch of earth, Gerard began sketching lines in the dirt with the tip of his butcher knife. It took just a few strokes for Ethan to recognize the winding course of the Marias, the breaks and coulées that marked the river south of Sundance.

"Here," Gerard said, making a series of Xs, "is Sundance, no? Here is Kestler's Lazy-K, and here the Bar-Five. And here"—he stabbed at the dirt—"are the homes of Handleman and Emile and Ian McMillan. Four men killed, counting Jacob, and now these places where they lived are empty . . . except for the Bar-Five. Even so, Victor has been shot, Ben and Joel are in jail, and you"—he looked at Ethan—"you slip around town like a coyote, afraid to be seen."

"Afraid he'll be shot," Seth corrected.

"All these men, all these homes that are now empty." A smile tugged at the corners of his lips when he saw the sudden look of understanding come over Ethan's face. "You see it, yes?"

"Yeah, I see it."

He'd seen it earlier too, on the map in Jeff Burke's office, but he hadn't put it together because a vital piece of the puzzle was still missing. Now, with Handleman's murder, that piece had been dropped neatly into place—an arch that ran north through the breaks of the Marias, the town of Sundance at its apex. But he saw something else, too, something Gerard hadn't included.

Dropping to one knee, Ethan lifted the knife gently from Gerard's hands and drew a straight line across the base of the sketch, south of the Marias.

"*Sacre bleu!*" Francois exploded.

Taking a clay pipe from his mouth, Scotty Dunham said: "Aye, we should 'a' seen it, lads. The damn' railroad."

Gerard's eyes seemed to glitter as he ran a hand, magician-like, above the map. "These lands . . . for the railroad they would be easy to grade, no? See, here above old Emile's cabin, then down along the river to Jacob's and across the Marias there. Then the same going west, where the bluffs are lower, the land not so broken. Here, between where Ian and Tom had their cabins." He stood, returned the knife to its sheath. "But who would do such a thing, and why? Except for Jacob, no one had claim to the land. No one owned it. The railroad could have paid each of these men a few dollars and they would have moved on just to get away from the noise."

"Except for Jacob," Badger Dick reminded them.

"*Oui*, except for Jacob." François looked at Ethan. "So, as Gerard says . . . who, my young friend?"

"Somebody who plans to make a legal claim on that land, then sell it to the railroad for a lot more than a few dollars."

"Ah," Gerard said, suddenly understanding. "For money."

"What else?" Scotty replied sarcastically.

"Then our duty is as it was before," Gerard continued. "We look for the men who killed Ian and his woman, and now Tom Handleman."

"I've got a pretty good idea who's doing the killing," Ethan said.

Scotty's eyes widened. "Ye know his name, do ye?"

"If it's who I think it is, his name is Nolan Andrews, and he's got a bunch of hardcases riding for him."

"Andrews?" Gerard repeated. "The man you fought in Ira Webb's saloon?"

"He wanted to buy the Bar-Five, but Pa wouldn't sell it. He came up to me in the Bullshead the day I got back from the high country. I expect he was hoping I'd talk Pa into changing his mind. When I refused, he tried to goad me into a fight, wanted me to draw my pistol against him. If Ira hadn't been there, I might've done it."

"If you had, then I think you would now be dead, my friend," François opined soberly.

Ethan nodded silent agreement, icy tendrils of comprehension entwining the base of his spine as he realized how close he'd come to falling into Andrews's trap. At the time, he hadn't even seen it.

"So, 'tis Andrews we're looking for?" Scotty asked.

"Not just him," Ethan said. "Andrews isn't a businessman, he's a killer. We're looking for someone else, someone with money and connections, especially to the railroad." He stared distractedly at Gerard's map, brows furrowed. "Andrews told me he was working for an outfit out of Bismarck called Westminster Cattle and Mining. Claimed they were wanting to expand onto the northern ranges."

"An outfit like that'd have some big money backin' 'em," Badger Dick said. "But would it have the connections? That'd have to be someone local, someone who knows the breaks and us that lived there. That's the person I want, boys. The dirty cuss who hired Andrews and his hardcases."

"*Oui*," Gerard agreed. "It is that one who must be stopped, else more killers will be brought in. So, again." He glanced at Ethan. "Who?"

"I don't know."

"Kestler?" Gabe ventured.

"Charlie?" Scotty sounded dubious. "Sure, and what would Charlie Kestler have to gain from killing the likes o' us? Hell, we be the ones keepin' the wolf population under control so he can run his damn' cows all up and down the river."

"It could be anyone," Ethan remarked. "I'm not saying it is Kestler, but I wouldn't put it past him, either. Not the way he's been yammering for Joel and Ben's hides."

"Andrews," Gerard said reflectively. "Where is he now?"

"I haven't seen him. His men were in town earlier, but they seemed to have disappeared when Kestler and his boys showed up."

"Then I think we should find them."

"They've been keeping their horses at Palmer's, in the nearest pen behind the main stables. Be easy enough to check if they're still there."

"*Oui*, if their horses are there, then they are still in town." François glanced at Hank McKay. "What do you say, gabby? You will come with me to check these horses?"

"I will," McKay growled.

He and François disappeared.

Gerard looked at Ethan. "While they are gone maybe there is someone you wish to speak with? Someone who wishes to speak to you."

Ethan smiled his gratitude. "I won't be long."

Gerard remained with the others as Ethan headed for the Turcotte wagon.

Rachel rose from the fire as he approached, hurried to his side. "Ethan," she said, taking his arm in both of hers and pulling it close. "I am so sorry. How is Victor?"

"He was better the last time I saw him, but he's got a bullet near his heart and Doc Carver is afraid to dig it out."

Rachel's face scrunched up in worry. "Will he . . . ?"

"I don't know." A shiver racked Ethan's body, like a fever chill. He tried to laugh it off but Rachel wouldn't let him.

"It is OK to be afraid for your brothers," she said, "and to feel pain for your father's death. You have suffered much these last few days."

"Why did you come?" Ethan asked in an attempt to change the subject, then immediately regretted it. "I'm sorry. I didn't mean to sound like I wasn't glad to see you. It's just that there's a lot of fired-up feelings right now, and I don't want you to get hurt."

"What would you have me do, Ethan? Stay at home? Hide under my blankets like a frightened child? I can shoot, and I can fight if I have to."

"I know. I was wrong."

Her eyes searched his. "Tell me the truth. Are you glad I came, or do you want me to go away? I will do as you wish."

"I want you to be safe, because, if you were injured or . . . or killed, I don't think I could take it." The words came out simply, yet with a gut-deep honesty that caught him off guard. He caressed her cheek with the backs of his fingers. "I love you, Rachel, but I don't know what's going to happen. There are too many factions involved. We're not even sure who our enemy is yet."

She placed a hand over his, the other on his chest. "It doesn't matter, Ethan. I will be here, waiting. Or I will go home to wait if you wish. But I would rather stand at your side, armed. I could use Papa's shotgun. . . ."

"No. I want you to stay here. Wait for me here." He looked toward the fire where Corn Grower stood watching them. Rachel lowered her hands.

"We should go back. Mama watches, and . . . I think she knows."

Ethan remembered the look Corn Grower had given him that morning at the Turcotte cabin, the conversation he'd had with Gerard on top of the bluff overlooking the Marias. He thought Rachel was probably right. They knew, and they would tolerate only so much. Taking her hand in his, he said: "Let's go over to the fire and greet your mother, and not give her anything else to worry about."

Chapter Fourteen

Darkness fell, and a cold, blustery wind kicked up out of the northwest, pummeling the fire at Badger Dick's wagon, nipping at Ethan's nose and fingers. His heavy coat was back at the ranch; a canvas jacket wrapped in the bedroll behind his saddle on the Appaloosa might as well have been. He wished now he hadn't refused Rachel's offer of a Hudson's Bay blanket to drape over his shoulders while he waited with the others for François LaBarge and Hank McKay to return from town.

Standing slightly apart from the others, Ethan only became aware of a presence moving up behind him at the last minute. His hand streaked to his revolver, but he was too slow. A second hand clamped on top of his, trapping the Remington in its holster.

In his ear, Seth Barlow chuckled good-naturedly. "You grow careless, Ethan. Not so long ago, I couldn't have gotten within twenty feet of you without being heard."

"That must be it," Ethan replied, forcing a lop-sided grin he didn't feel.

At the fire, the older men looked up, a couple of them chuckling at Ethan's expense. Then they turned their backs to the younger men, and Seth gave Ethan a nudge.

"Come with me."

Ethan followed the young hunter away from the wagons.

Gabe waited for them in the dark with Ethan's rifle and shell belt. He handed them over, then turned away without speaking.

"Where are we going?" Ethan asked, buckling the belt around his waist.

"Me 'n' Gabe's been doing a little scouting," Seth replied, falling in beside Ethan. "You'll see."

Although curious, Ethan held his tongue. They backtracked through Sundance's alleys and rear lots as far as the Bullshead. Here, Gabe held up a hand. Ethan stopped, but Seth kept walking.

"We'll wait over there," Gabe said, nodding toward a harness shop north of the saloon, separated from it by an empty, weed-choked lot.

The two men moved cautiously through the lot, keeping to the shadows as much as possible. Reaching a position close to the street, they settled down behind a stack of discarded lumber where they had a clear view of the boardwalk in front of the Bullshead.

Ethan's nerves were jangled as he studied the crowd. Horsemen rode back and forth on the street, and now and then someone would fire his revolver toward the sky, the clap of gunfire disconcerting. A couple of whiskey-sodden cowhands jogged their mounts into the lot, so close that Ethan could have touched the stirrup of the nearest rider. He recognized the slack face of the short cowhand from the saloon that morning, one of the men who had tried to prevent Ethan from leaving. In the flickering torchlight, Ethan would have sworn the drunken cowboy was looking straight at him, but then he reined away without raising an alarm.

"What are we doing here?" Ethan whispered tersely.

"Waiting."

"For what?"

Gabe nodded toward the boardwalk. "Watch."

Ethan looked. Seth was approaching the saloon's batwing doors from the south, threading his way casually through a mob of drinking cowboys. The crowd was boisterous, their laughter raking the night like spurs, but Ethan could sense an undertone of hostility in their crude jokes and rough-housing. They were

141

killing time, bulking up on courage from bottles of Ira's cheap river whiskey—just as Charlie Kestler seemingly wanted it.

There were no townspeople in sight, and Ethan doubted if any of them had lingered much past sunset as the cowhands grew more unruly, the night more dangerous. They would retreat to their homes, he thought bitterly, there to blow out their lamps and cower in fear until dawn brought an end to the tempest.

As Seth glided into the lamplight that spilled out over the tops of the batwings, the crowd turned abruptly silent. A cowboy with a drooping mustache and a sneering frown stepped into his path.

"Hol' on there, redskin. Where yuh goin'?"

"I'm looking for someone," Seth replied calmly, making no attempt to push past the cowboy.

The Lazy-K hand seemed to ponder Seth's reply. Then he looked at the men surrounding him and laughed. "Ah hate tuh tell yuh this, sonny, but they ain't no someone 'round here, and old man Webb don't serve liquor to Injuns."

Several of the men laughed loudly, but others didn't; the threat of violence seemed almost palpable. Ethan shifted uneasily, ready to go to Seth's aid, but Gabe stopped him with a touch.

"Wait. Let's see what happens."

Seth hadn't budged. "I'm looking for Nate Kestler."

"Nate?" The cowboy's eyes narrowed suspiciously. "What duh yuh want with Natey?"

"I have a message for him."

The cowboy's face screwed up with uncertainty. "What kinda message?"

"From a friend."

"Maybe he does," another cowboy interjected.

"They know about Janey," Gabe whispered to Ethan.

Janey, with her Indian blood, Seth with his. It would make sense to a bunch of drunken cowhands.

The first cowboy was shaking his head negatively. "Why'd some redskin want tuh get a message to Nate tonight?"

Seth shrugged and started to turn away. "It doesn't matter. I can tell him tomorrow . . . if it isn't too late."

"Now, jus' hol' on," the first cowboy said, grabbing Seth's arm and pulling him back. "I ain't made up muh mind about yuh yet."

Seth smiled reasonably. "Maybe when you're sober."

"I'm sober enough now," the cowboy said, bristling, but, when several of the men nearby laughed, the cowboy's face turned red. "The hell wit' it. Go on, skedaddle."

"What about my message for Nate?"

The cowboy was blinking rapidly. "Yuh go on 'n' wait over there outta the way." He pointed vaguely toward the harness shop. "I'll tell Nate yuh wanna talk to 'im. If he wants tuh talk to yuh, I reckon he'll come find yuh."

Ethan breathed a sigh of relief, his fingers relaxing their tight grip on the Winchester.

On the boardwalk, Seth said: "I'll be around back. He can find me there, if he doesn't take too long."

"Yeah, yeah, I'll tell 'im," the cowboy said, giving Seth a light shove. "Go on now, git. White men's tryin' tuh have a littl' fun."

Seth passed through the crowd to the empty lot north of the saloon. No one tried to stop him; they wouldn't now, with Nate involved.

Ethan and Gabe waited until the first cowboy disappeared inside, then slipped out from behind the stacked lumber. They caught up with Seth in back of the saloon, filling his pipe from a brain-tanned tobacco pouch, but didn't approach him.

"Over here," Gabe said, backing up to the rear wall of the saddlery.

It didn't take long for Nate Kestler to show. Ethan heard a couple of men tramping through the weedy lot several seconds before he saw them. They moved clumsily, stumbling over empty bottles and discarded tins. The cowboy who had gone to fetch Nate cursed the uneven footing. A second voice said: "Shut up, Maynard."

Ethan smiled thinly. That was Nate, all right.

"Who's over there?" Nate Kestler demanded, coming to a stop only a few feet away from where Ethan and Gabe were standing.

"Seth Barlow," Seth replied. "I have a message."

"Well, out with it," Nate said impatiently.

"For the world to hear?" Seth asked mildly. He struck a match to light his pipe, turning his back to the wind and cupping his hands tightly around the tiny, sputtering flame.

Nate cursed and started forward. The cowboy followed. Gabe and Ethan stepped after them. Not nearly as inebriated as his partner, Nate sensed their presence almost immediately, but Gabe was on him before he could shout a warning. The cowboy didn't have a clue anyone else was around, and crumbled silently under a roundhouse blow from the Winchester's butt. Seth shook out his match without lighting his pipe and came over. Ethan and Gabe hauled Nate to his feet, a wadded piece of gunny sacking already shoved into his mouth. Ethan plucked the revolvers from Nate's holsters and tossed them into the weeds.

"This way," Seth ordered, and, with Nate struggling between them, Ethan and Gabe hustled him away from the saloon.

They went to Carver's barn, slipping in through the back door, and Seth struck another match to light a lantern.

"You've been here before," Ethan remarked.

"This afternoon," Seth confessed. "Me 'n' Gabe came looking for a likely spot when we hatched this idea."

Nate kicked at Seth, but Gabe jerked him off balance and threw him to the ground. Pulling a short length of rope from his belt, he said: "Flop him on his belly, Ethan, so I can tie his hands."

It took only moments to truss up Nate like a hog for market. Gabe hauled him roughly to his feet, then marched him over to a feed box and made him sit down. Pulling a knife from its sheath, he held it against Nate's throat.

"Do you believe I'll kill you?" he asked menacingly.

144

Nate snorted in disdain; he wasn't buying it.

Lifting the knife from Gabe's hand, Ethan leaned close. "What about me, pissant? Do you believe I'll slit your worthless throat?" He pushed the knife's tip into the soft tissue of Nate's neck until a trickle of blood ran down into his collar.

Feeling the warm flow, Nate tried to pull away, but Gabe held him tight. In that same low, deadly tone, Ethan said: "My old man is dead and Vic is dying, and now that son-of-a-bitch you call a father wants to hang Joel and Ben. So what about it, Kestler? Do you believe I'd just as soon cut your throat as look at you?"

This time, Nate nodded with enthusiasm.

Grabbing the sacking that protruded from between the younger man's lips, Ethan said: "I'm going to pull this gag out. If you even try to shout for help, you're a dead man." Nate's head bobbed acknowledgment, and Ethan yanked the coarse cloth from his mouth.

Nate drew in a ragged breath, but didn't make a peep otherwise.

"For someone who carries two pistols, you caved awfully fast," Seth observed.

"What do you want?" Nate demanded angrily.

Gabe rapped him upside his head. "Only speak when you're spoken to, shithead."

Leaning forward until they were practically nose to nose, Ethan said: "Who killed Jacob Wilder?"

"I don't know."

Gabe cuffed him once more, a mother bear disciplining its cub. "Tell the truth or I'll smack you till your ears ring like bells."

"You big, dumb bastard," Nate spat, earning himself a third quick slap to the side of his head.

"Ethan, I don't think this boy believes us," Seth remarked. "Mind if I borrow that sticker?" Ethan handed him the knife. Seth brought the tip up into Nate's left nostril. "Maybe we ought to notch him," he said.

"Take off the whole damn' nose," Gabe urged.

"I'd rather he talk," Ethan said. "If we cut off too much, he's liable to pass out."

"You boys are crazy," Nate said. "Do you think my men don't know I'm missing? What do you think they'll do when they find out what happened?"

"First off," Seth corrected, "they're your daddy's men, not yours, and I truly doubt if they'll notice or even care what happens to some little coyote who sneaks around peeping on good girls like Janey Handleman. Far as they're concerned, you ain't nothing but an embarrassment to the Lazy-K, a patch of alkali on your daddy's range. And second"—Seth pressed upward on the blade, forcing Nate's head back against the wall—"second, it won't matter what they do. You'll still be walking around without a nose."

Nate's eyes slowly widened in belief.

"We're wasting time," Ethan said bluntly. "Nate, you start talking or I'll cut it off myself."

"I don't know anything," Nate insisted.

"Maybe we ought to take off an ear, instead," Seth said, moving the knife around to the side of the younger man's head. He made a quick slicing motion, and a spout of blood arched into the barn's entry.

When Nate started to squawk, Gabe hurriedly shoved the sacking back into his mouth.

"Tell us!" Seth shouted into Nate's face. "Tell us, or by God, I'll cut both ears off."

Nate struggled desperately, but Gabe's grip was too strong. Seth passed the bloodied knife in front of Nate's eyes, on its way to the other ear. A fresh spurt of blood, and Nate screamed into the sacking. "Talk, boy!" Seth roared.

Nate was jerking wildly, tears streaming down his cheeks. They waited until his gyrations slowed before Gabe removed the sacking. "Please, God, don't cut me no more," Nate blubbered.

Ethan shoved forward. "Who hired Nolan Andrews and his boys?"

"I don't . . . Jesus, no!" He strained away from the knife Seth brandished in his face. "I'll tell you, I'll tell you! Just . . . give me a minute . . ."

"Bullshit," Seth spat. "Let's gag him again and whittle off something else."

Nate threw Ethan a desperate look. "I swear, Wilder, I'll tell you everything I know, but I don't know who hired Andrews. I swear to God I don't!"

"What do you know?"

Nate swallowed hard, tried to calm himself. "I . . . not much. Pa never tells me anything, just 'be here' or 'go there.' All I know is what I overhear."

"Nate," Ethan said darkly.

"All right, I . . . I heard him talking to Finch tonight."

"Ralph Finch, Burke's deputy?"

"Yeah. Pa said he'd make it worth Finch's while if he got us into the jail. Said there'd be enough for him to go somewhere else and live good for a year, never have to lift a finger."

"What did Finch say?"

"He said he'd do it, and took off just a couple of minutes before Maynard came in. I figured . . ."

Ethan swore and spun away from the rancher's son, heading for the door.

"Ethan, what do you want us to do with . . . ?" Seth called.

"Do whatever you want with him," Ethan snapped.

The wind was growing stronger, kicking up skiffs of dust that it flung about randomly, and lightning flashed in the distance. The air felt charged and heady, like the night itself was about to explode.

Ethan stopped at the edge of the street in front of Carver's house. Down at the Bullshead, Charlie Kestler was sitting his horse in impatient fury, jerking at the bit with a tight rein, gouging the animal with his spurs, then pulling it back. Most of his crew were already mounted, but a few of them were still afoot, scurrying about in different directions as if searching for someone.

Searching for Nate, Ethan thought. Unknowingly he and the Barlows had bought themselves some time when they snatched Nate out of the Bullshead's back lot, but he knew Charlie wouldn't wait forever.

Keeping out of sight, Ethan hurried toward the jail. The sounds of unrest in the street grew louder as he drew closer. Torches bucked in the strengthening wind. He was just entering the alley behind the jail when the rear door flew open and Finch came running out. The two men nearly collided. Finch's eyes saucered when he recognized Ethan. He opened his mouth as if to cry a warning, but Ethan, carrying his rifle in both hands, instinctively swung the butt upward as hard as he could. The blow caught Finch under the chin and the deputy crumpled as if someone had pulled a pin loosening every joint in his body.

Ethan hesitated only a moment. Then he heard a crash from the front of the jail, and knew that Charlie Kestler had come for his revenge.

Chapter Fifteen

Leaving Finch in a heap outside, Ethan raced into the jail just as a second mighty blow shook the building. He'd expected the front door to be unlocked, but either Finch had forgotten to throw the bolt, or he'd panicked and fled before completing his assignment.

Jeff Burke lay on the floor beside his desk, the hair on the back of his head matted with seeping blood, while men out front yelled for him to open up, threatening to tear the door off its hinges if he didn't comply. Ethan wondered how many of them knew about Kestler's bribe, Finch's double-cross.

The keys to the cells were hung on a peg beside the door leading into the holding area. Ethan grabbed them on his way through. The faces of both Joel and Ben were pressed to the bars, ashen with fear.

"Ethan!" Ben shouted.

"Shut up," Joel snapped.

"Both of you shut up," Ethan ordered. He unlocked Joel's cell first. "You remember what I said about horses?"

"You've got two of 'em saddled and waiting in Carver's barn."

Ethan shoved the big .50-95 Winchester into Joel's hands. "Take this . . . just don't use it if you don't have to." He went to the next cell and released Ben. "Stay with Joel," he ordered. "Head up to Elk Camp. I'll find you there. And dammit, Ben, do what I say this time!"

"I will," Ben promised as Ethan hustled him down the hall after Joel.

They passed through the front room. Jeff was coming around, up on his elbows with his head wagging groggily. There was more pounding at the front door, and the jamb suddenly splintered, revealing a long, jagged scar in the wood. Ethan grabbed Jeff's collar and hauled him to his feet. The sheriff made a feeble attempt to draw his revolver but his holster was empty, the gun nowhere in sight.

"Get your hands off me, Wilder," Jeff said, but it was a command without teeth. The way the sheriff was wobbling, Ethan figured the lawman would drop like a rock if he did.

"Come with me," Ethan said, propelling Jeff toward the cells. "Kestler's liable to shoot you if he busts in here and you try to stop him."

"I can handle . . ." The sheriff's words trailed off. Ethan led him into a cell, then slammed the door shut and turned the lock. ". . . Charlie Kestler," Jeff finished finally, slumping down on the bunk. "Jesus," he whispered, bowing his head to the pain.

"It's better this way," Ethan assured him.

Then the whole building shuddered under a massive blow, and Ethan darted back into the office. The front door was partially down, nearly torn from its frame. Only the lower hinge was holding, but that wasn't enough to keep out Kestler's men.

Clint, the tall cowboy from the Bullshead, was the first to scramble inside; the shorter cowboy followed. Kestler was the third man back, urging those in front of him to hurry, but the twisted door kept teetering under them, throwing them off balance. Then Kestler spotted Ethan.

"It's Wilder!" he screamed. "Shoot the bastard!"

The door lurched suddenly, and Clint dropped, hard, to one knee, nearly losing his revolver. The second cowboy continued to take aim, but clumsily.

Ethan palmed his Remington and snapped off a shot that thudded into the jamb next to the cowboy's head. The cowboy cried out and jerked away, splinters angling from his cheek like tiny spears. Then the door shifted once more and his feet slid out from under him. He fell on top of Clint and the two men tumbled into the jail. Kestler had a clear shot now, and Ethan ducked as the rancher fired. He felt a child-like tug at his shirt, a brief sting, then he was retreating toward the back door, firing rapidly.

Powder smoke filled the sheriff's office, obscuring everyone's view. Ethan didn't know if he'd hit anyone or not, but he made it to the rear door unscathed. Leaping Finch's prone form, he sprinted into the darkness of the alley. Gunfire continued to puncture the night, but the sounds of battle softened after Ethan put several buildings between himself and the jail.

His pulse thundered in his ears as he made his way back to the Carvers'. He walked swiftly, reloading as he went. The old cap-and-ball revolver was slow to charge, but he'd done it a thousand times before, and was barely aware that he was doing it now. He capped all six chambers, then lowered the hammer to a safety notch cut between the nipples.

Carver's home, like the rest of the town save for the Bullshead and the sheriff's office, was dark. Even the porch lamp Doc normally kept lit for injured parties to find his office after hours had been snuffed.

Ethan by-passed the house for the barn. The wide front door was open, and he paused outside to listen. Everything seemed quiet, and he slipped inside, revolver cocked. "Joel?" he whispered. "Ben?"

There was no answer.

"Seth?"

More silence. He remembered the lantern they'd used earlier, and felt his way to it. He was careful to stand well back from the match's flare when he scratched it alight, but there was no reaction. Lighting the lantern and raising it above his head, he spun a slow circle. There was nothing to see. The barn was empty.

He went over to where they'd bullied Nate Kestler into revealing his father's plan to break into the jail. There was blood on the straw, but not much, and the stalls were empty. The Appaloosa and sorrel were gone, and Ethan began to breathe easier.

He extinguished the lantern and left the barn, turning north toward the hunters' camp. Normally there would have been firelight to guide him, but the camp was dark in the face of the approaching storm—either the one coming in from the high plains with its distant lightning and gusting winds, or the one still brewing in town. He was almost upon the wagons before he could make them out, hulking shadows only slightly darker than the surrounding landscape. He stopped to listen but couldn't even make out the murmur of conversation. Wrapping his fingers around the Remington's smooth grips, Ethan eased toward Badger Dick's wagon.

He was almost at the tailgate before a solitary figure next to the rear wheel challenged his approach. "Who's there?"

"Ethan Wilder."

"By God, it's Ethan, boys!" Badger Dick exclaimed. "Come on in, son."

Ethan heard others coming toward him, shuffling feet, muted greetings, genuine happiness for his safe return. He wasn't surprised to see that they were all heavily armed. He'd expected no less.

"Where are Seth and Gabe?" he asked.

"Right here," Seth answered from nearby. He came up to clap Ethan on the shoulder. "We heard gunfire, and were afraid you'd been shot."

"I'm all right," Ethan replied, then told them what had happened at the jail.

When he finished, Gerard said: "Burke, he saw you break Joel and Ben out of jail?"

Ethan nodded, growing somber when he saw Gerard's worried expression. "Why? What's wrong?"

"You broke the law," Badger Dick said. "You'll be wanted by it now."

"Me?" Ethan stared at those around him. "I saved my brothers from a lynching. Jeff can't hold that against me."

"But Kestler can, and he's powerful enough to see that the reasons you did it get swept out the back door where no one can see them," Badger Dick replied.

"Maybe it will not be as we fear, but you cannot take that chance," Gerard said kindly.

Ethan swore under his breath, but he knew they were right. If Kestler wanted him out of the way, Ethan had just dropped the means to do it right in the cattleman's lap.

"Your horse, where is it?" Gerard asked.

"Joel and Ben have them."

"Gabe, fetch Pokey," Badger Dick told his son. "Ethan, you have to get out of Sundance, at least for a while. Go find your brothers at Elk Camp."

"You know about Elk Camp?"

Badger Dick smiled. "Of course we know about Elk Camp. Where else would a Wilder go when he's in trouble?"

Gabe returned within minutes, leading a tall horse already saddled and bridled.

"Woman!" Badger Dick called in a low voice, and Mary Many Robes materialized out of the darkness, arms burdened with gear that she began stowing on the horse.

"There are some blankets and food and my bear-hide coat," Badger Dick said. "Enough to keep you for a few days. I'll send Gabe or Seth when things settle down."

Ethan took the reins and stepped into the saddle.

"God give you speed," Gerard said.

Ethan nodded stiffly and reined away, jogging his mount over to Turcotte's wagon. He called out softly as he approached, and a shadow separated itself from the wagon and moved swiftly toward him.

"Ethan!" Rachel cried, and he stepped down and caught her in his arms. She wrapped hers around his neck, pulling his face close, pressing her lips to his with an unfamiliar hunger. "I was scared," she said, leaning back. "There was so much shooting."

"I'm all right, but I have to go away for a while."

"I know. I heard."

"Stay close to camp and don't go into town. Things are getting mean in there. Chances are I'll be back in a few days, but, if not, I'll get word to you somehow."

"Papa says you are wanted by the law, like Joel and Ben."

"Just for a while . . . just until Jeff gets back on his feet. Then I'll come in and we'll sort it all out."

Her arms tightened, her body so warm and soft he wanted to sink into it forever. "Be careful, Ethan. I love you."

He took her chin in his fingers, tipped her face up, lowered his. There was a tenderness in their kiss that had not been there before, a knowledge that this moment might never be repeated.

Breaking it, he said: "I love you, too, Rachel."

"Ethan!"

He swung into the saddle and rode away.

Chapter Sixteen

He watched the house from the cover of the barn. The windows were dark, the street silent. Even the ruckus down by the jail had tapered off to a grumbling echo. After half an hour, he left his roost to glide stealthily across the rear yard. When he knocked at the door, a voice answered immediately, demanding identification.

"Ethan Wilder."

The lock turned and the door swung inward. "Come in," Doc said tersely.

Ethan entered the dimly lit room, and Carver shut and locked the door. There was a lamp on the desk, its wick turned so low it barely illuminated the room, and heavy drapes on the windows had been drawn closed.

"What happened out there?" he asked.

Ethan told him some of it—his attempt to talk Ira into closing the Bullshead, his visit to the hunters' camp, followed by his encounter at the jail with Charlie Kestler—but left out the parts about threatening Nate Kestler in Doc's barn, and smacking Ralph Finch upside his head with a rifle butt.

There was a rustle of satin at the parlor door and Claudia came into the office, her expression grave. "Was anyone hurt?" she asked, leading Ethan to believe she had been listening from the other room.

"Jeff took a hard rap to the top of his head."

"Does he need help?" Doc asked.

"I reckon if he does, he'll know where to find it."

"Ethan is right," Claudia said. "You should stay here. This will be where they will bring anyone who needs your assistance."

She made sense, Ethan thought, but he could tell Doc was torn. He wanted to go where he was needed; he just wasn't sure where that was at the moment.

"I'll stay for a while," he said finally.

"How's Vic?" Ethan asked.

Doc exchanged a strained look with his wife, then sighed. "I'm afraid Vic relapsed this evening."

"Relapsed? What does . . . is he dying?"

"You knew how seriously injured Vic was," Doc replied almost defensively. "Most men wouldn't have survived the ride into town."

"But you said he was getting better."

"No, I didn't. Vic rallied briefly this afternoon, but he never fully regained consciousness. Not even when you were speaking with him." Doc walked over to a wing-back leather chair and seemed to collapse within its embrace. There was a bottle of bourbon and a tumbler on the little table beside him, the tumbler containing maybe a quarter inch of liquor. He drained it swiftly, then grimaced and set the glass aside. Shaking his head at his helplessness, he said: "There's nothing I can do. I don't have the skills to attempt the kind of operation your brother needs."

Ethan glanced at the bottle. Doc made a dismissing gesture in its direction. "It's not that. It's . . . I'm not a young man any more. My hands aren't as steady as they used to be, and my vision isn't as sharp. With the location of the bullet, and especially the bone fragments, even a twitch on my part during surgery could kill him."

"Mister Carver seldom drinks," Claudia said in her husband's behalf. "He's had that same bottle of bourbon since last Christmas."

Ethan lumbered over to a chair in front of Doc's desk and sat down heavily. He felt suddenly exhausted, as if everything that had happened since his return from the mountains had caught up with him in that instant. "Is there anyone who can operate on him?"

"Perhaps in Bismarck or Saint Paul. Most certainly there would be qualified surgeons in Chicago. But the risk in transporting Vic there would negate the odds of success to practically zero, and I frankly doubt if a younger, more skilled physician would come here. Especially in light of your brother's current condition. The odds that he'd live long enough for help to arrive are slim."

"But there is a chance?"

Doc hesitated, then shook his head. "No. I'm sorry."

Ethan tipped his head back and closed his eyes. He wanted to sleep, to cry; he wanted to rip and tear and bellow his rage. But he did none of that. He forced himself to remain seated, to keep his mouth shut, palms flat on his knees.

"You can sit with him if you'd like," Doc said.

"No, maybe later." Slowly, as if carrying a hundred-pound sack of grain on each shoulder, Ethan stood and headed for the door.

"Where are you going?"

"Gerard Turcotte pointed out that I might be in trouble with the law for busting Joel and Ben out of jail. They figure I ought to head for the mountains for a while, wait until things cool off."

"No," Claudia protested.

Doc, though, was more pragmatic. "It's possible, dear. Ethan did break the law, no matter how worthwhile the cause."

She stared at her husband in disbelief. "And there is nothing we can do?"

"At the moment, I don't think so. Tomorrow, when things have calmed down, I'll talk to the sheriff. Jeff is a reasonable man."

"I'd appreciate that, Doc," Ethan said.

"You have food and bedding?"

"Yes, sir, I do."

"I'll talk to Gerard after I've talked to Jeff," Doc promised. "He can let you know what I find out."

Ethan nodded and cracked open the door. Spying nothing out of the ordinary, he slipped through the door and crossed to the barn, where he'd left his borrowed horse. Backing it out of the same stall where he'd kept the Appaloosa, he was just stretching his toe for the stirrup when a voice stopped him cold.

"Going somewhere, Ethan?"

He lowered his foot, reins in one hand, cantle in the other. When he started to lower his arms, the voice said: "Uhn-uh, keep your hands where I can see them."

"I didn't do anything wrong, Jeff," Ethan said. "Kestler and his boys were coming through the front door and you were flat on the floor."

"So you killed my deputy and broke your brothers out of jail, and now you're riding out after them."

Ethan turned slowly. "What do you mean . . . killed your deputy?"

"I mean just what I said. You stuck a knife between Ralph Finch's ribs, then set your brothers free."

"I didn't stick Ralph with a knife. He was still alive when I left the jail."

"Then one of your brothers did it."

Ethan thought back to the scene in the alley behind the jail. He'd been moving fast, exiting the rear door, gunfire from Kestler and his men still barking the quiet off the night. He remembered leaping Finch's body, looking down as he passed over the deputy's prostrate form. He didn't remember a knife, yet supposed he could have missed it. As dark as it was, everything happening so fast, a knife buried hilt-deep in a man's ribs would have been an easy thing to miss.

"What did it look like?" Ethan asked. "The knife, I mean."

"You tell me."

"Ben carries a camp knife with a Sheffield mark. Joel carries a folder with a three-inch blade. I'm guessing you still have both of them stowed away somewhere in your office."

Jeff stepped out of an empty stall. "There's a lantern hanging on a hook beside your head. Light it."

Ethan did as he was told, then stepped away from his horse—another bay, he saw for the first time.

Jeff moved into the light with a cocked, double-barreled shotgun pointed at Ethan's stomach. "Let me see your knife," he said. "Slowly."

Ethan pulled the short Bowie from its sheath and handed it over, butt first. Jeff took it, studied the blade a moment, then lifted it to his nose to sniff the hammered steel. Satisfied, he handed it back. "It wasn't that one."

"I already know that," Ethan said, feeling a glimmer of hope. "You remember that it was Finch who cold-cocked you, don't you?"

Jeff hesitated, then shook his head. "All I remember is Kestler and his men coming for your brothers. The next thing I know, I'm sitting in a locked cell with Charlie opening the door for me. He said you killed Ralph, then knocked me over the head so you could free Joel and Ben."

"That's not true. I broke Joel and Ben out, all right, but it was Finch who slugged you."

"You saw him do it?"

"No, but I ran into him in the alley behind the jail and gave him a good smack with my rifle butt. Finch was double-crossing you, Jeff. That's why I was there, to stop him."

Jeff's eyes narrowed suspiciously. "How do you figure that?"

"Nate Kestler told me."

"Nate? Nate Kestler just . . ."

"We had to worm it out of him," Ethan explained.

"We?"

"Me."

"Ethan, you're in enough trouble right now. Don't make it worse with lies."

"I'm not looking to cause any more trouble than this town's already got. I caught Nate behind the Bullshead and roughed him up a little to make him tell me what's been going on around here lately. That's when he told me he'd overheard his old man talking to Ralph, offering him money to get you out of the way."

The shotgun's muzzles came down partway. "That little weasel. He would've done it, too. But that doesn't explain how he got a knife in his ribs."

"It wasn't me, and I doubt if it was Joel or Ben. We were all moving pretty fast."

"Then you're implying Kestler or one of his men did it?"

"I don't know what happened to Finch, but if he did take that money so my brothers could hang, then I don't really care."

"You'd better care," Jeff said. "Because right now, Kestler and his men are saying you did it, and I'm bound to believe them if I can't find proof that says otherwise."

"You might be bound to it, but I don't think you do. You wouldn't have given me my knife if you thought I'd killed your deputy with it."

Exhaling loudly, Jeff lowered the shotgun the rest of the way. "No, I don't think you did it, but I do wonder where you're going now."

"To find Joel and Ben."

"You know where they are?"

Ethan shrugged vaguely. "I might."

"All right, I'm not going to push it, but I want you to go get them, bring them back."

"To hang?"

"To face the charges that were originally brought against them." Jeff's voice softened. "Bring 'em in, Ethan. Let's get this mess straightened out before anyone else is killed."

Ethan took up the reins to his horse. "I'll be back as soon as I can."

Chapter Seventeen

For all its rumbling thunder and flash lightning, it never did rain that night. Still, Ethan was glad for Badger Dick's heavy bear-hide coat. When dawn finally broke across the plains the next morning, there was frost everywhere, the short buffalo grass white as fresh-fallen snow.

The land here rolled gently, broken only by twisting draws and the distant line of the Rocky Mountains, still a day's ride to the west. Ethan kept his borrowed mount to a steady, mile-eating jog, its breath puffing like a straggled gray beard.

He paused long enough, when the sun came up, to dig some jerked venison and cold pan bread from his saddlebags. It was a far cry from last night's supper with the Carvers, but he ate what he had with relish, washing it down afterward with water from his canteen. He'd been in the saddle six hours already, and hoped to make Elk Camp before sundown.

Nothing stirred in all that vast expanse of high plains until just before noon, when a covey of prairie chickens shot out of the grass two hundred yards away. The bay snorted and threw up its head, and Ethan reached for his revolver. When a man's head appeared above the lip of a shallow draw near where the prairie chickens had taken flight, Ethan let his hand fall away from his sidearm. Pulling up, he waited for Joel and Ben to lope their horses to him.

"What are you doing out here?" Ben shouted while still a hundred yards away.

Joel snapped something at the younger man that Ethan couldn't hear, and Ben replied: "Heck, ain't no one out here gonna hear us."

They rode up—Joel grim-faced and haggard, Ben smiling like a kid with a pocketful of candy.

"You bring us anything to eat?" Ben asked, drawing rein. "You forgot to put any food in your saddlebags."

Joel shook his head in disgust. "I forgot how much that kid can jabber when he ain't distracted by something like a hangman's rope."

"I'm hungry," Ben protested. "We saw an antelope earlier, but Joel was afraid to shoot it. Said someone might hear us."

"He was right," Ethan said, dismounting and digging through the supplies Mary Many Robes had sent along. He passed out pieces of jerky and bread, then stood back to watch them eat. Joel had Ethan's .50-95 Winchester balanced across his saddlebows, but he was also carrying a revolver tucked inside the waistband of his trousers. Ethan cocked his head curiously.

"Where'd you get the wheel gun?"

Joel gave him a chary look. "It's mine."

"Huh! Ain't, either," Ben said. "He took it offa Ralph Finch, out back of the jail."

"That Finch's pistol?" Ethan asked pointedly.

Joel shifted a strip of jerky to his left hand, let his right come down close to the revolver. "It's mine now, and poor enough pay for the crap we put up with while we were locked up."

"He spit in our food," Ben added solemnly. "Laughed about it, too. Me 'n' Joel's gonna whale the tar outta that boy when this other business is settled."

Ethan studied Joel closely, but couldn't read anything except stubbornness in the younger man's expression. "I reckon you've both missed your opportunity," he said. "I talked to Jeff Burke last night, and Finch is dead."

"Dead," Ben echoed. "What did you do to him, Ethan?"

"I didn't do anything to him," Ethan replied irritably. "Somebody knifed him."

There was no immediate response to that. Ethan continued to watch Joel's face for any telltale sign of guilt, but saw nothing. It was Ben who broke the strained silence. "*Whoowee*," he said softly. "I knowed folks didn't like 'im, but I never figured he had enemies that'd want to kill 'im."

"Maybe he owed somebody money," Joel said, mulishly returning Ethan's stare.

"Or somebody owed him money and didn't want to pay it," Ethan suggested.

"Maybe he spit into somebody's food once too often," Ben added. "I'd've been tempted to stick a knife in him myself, if I'd've had one handy. He laughed when he did it, Ethan. That ain't right."

"Ralph Finch wasn't the sharpest blade on the butcher's block," Joel opined. "Likely the squirt here is right. Somebody got a chance to pay him back, and did."

"That's possible," Ethan agreed, stepping into the saddle of his borrowed horse.

"You figure it was something else?" Joel asked with an edge in his voice.

"Pull your horns in," Ethan said. "You're carrying Finch's revolver. Anybody sees it and knows what happened last night is naturally going to wonder."

"They can wonder all they want, long as they don't say anything about it where I can hear them. I've run plumb out of patience, big Brother, and I'm liable to bust a cap on the next son-of-a-bitch who tries to cross me today."

Ben gaped at Joel like he was a circus act. "What's got your hackles up?" he asked.

"I was damn' near hung last night," Joel snapped.

"Me, too," Ben replied, innocently puzzled.

Staying calm, Ethan said: "Yeah, but neither of you were hung, and I figure we've got trouble enough without one of you threatening to shoot the next guy who asks you a question."

"It ain't none of your business who I shoot," Joel said stonily.

Ethan sighed. "Shut up, Joel," he said wearily. "You're starting to sound like a magpie in a woodpile."

Ben chuckled. "About time someone else got told to shut up. What I wanna know is, where're we goin'?"

"I sure as hell ain't going to Elk Camp," Joel said. "We'd freeze our asses off up that high."

He eyed the bear-hide coat Ethan was wearing with envy. "That's what we need . . . some heavy clothes."

"And gloves," Ben added. "My fingers is freezin'."

"What we ought to do is ride back to Sundance and pay Sam Davidson a little visit," Joel said. "Outfit ourselves with better guns and some decent winter duds, then light a shuck for Canada and never look back."

"Run?" Ben said, gaze flitting between Ethan and Joel, lips speckled with crumbs. "Why should we run? We didn't do nothin'."

"It doesn't matter what we did or didn't do. If you still think Jeff Burke can keep our necks out of the noose after last night, you're an idiot."

"But this is our home," Ben said. "I don't want to leave." He looked at Ethan. "We ain't gonna run, are we?"

"No, we aren't." Ethan reined his horse around to face Joel. "I promised Jeff I'd bring the two of you back to Sundance. I aim to do it."

"Tell Burke you tried, but that I wouldn't come in," Joel replied. "Ben can go with you if he wants. I won't."

The muscles across the back of Ethan's skull drew taut. He could feel his own temper finally starting to bubble, patience stretched thin like rubber. He struggled to keep it under rein. "If you run now, Joel, it'll be the same as admitting you beat that girl. Is that what you want?"

"What I want is to not get my neck stretched for popping Suzie Merrick upside her head." He stopped abruptly, then shook his head. "I ain't saying I hit her, Ethan, but I am saying just about anybody would. She was making promises she had no intention of keeping, toying with me 'n' Nate Kestler like we were spiders on a string."

"Kestler isn't the one accused of beating her," Ethan reminded him.

Joel guffawed. "When his daddy is Charlie Kestler, the biggest rancher in these parts? Hell, no, she wouldn't accuse Natey."

There was a lot of truth in what Joel said, Ethan knew, but that wouldn't matter to the citizens of Sundance. If Joel ran now, they'd peg him guilty as surely as if he'd confessed. Shaking his head, he said: "I can't let you do it, Joel. If you take off, they'll say you're guilty, and just naturally assume Ben is, too."

Ben's eyes widened. "I don't wanna go back if they're gonna hang me, Ethan. I'd rather go with Joel than get lynched."

"I'm not going to let you run, Ben."

"It ain't your call, Eth," Joel said smugly. "Ben's fourteen, old enough to make his own decisions. If he wants to ride with me, I won't let you stop him."

"You threatening me, little Brother?"

"Call it what you want," Joel replied, moving his hand to the revolver tucked inside his waistband.

"Joel," Ben said uncertainly. "Don't do that."

"Shut up, Ben. I'm doing this for you." He started to slide the revolver from his waistband, yet seemed uncertain how far he could go before Ethan reacted.

Ethan didn't know the answer to that, either. Just the thought of going up against Joel in a gunfight made him feel nauseous. "Joel," he said finally, warningly.

"I mean it, Ethan. I'll shoot you before I go back."

"Joel!" Ben exclaimed.

"Shut up!" Joel shouted, yanking at his revolver while Ethan sat there with his own gun holstered, wondering if he was going to be shot down like a rabid dog by his own kin.

It was Ben, surprising all of them, who put a stop to Joel's draw. He'd been holding a canteen half filled with water and heavy as a blacksmith's hammer. When Joel started to pull his piece, Ben swung the canteen by its strap, bringing it over his horse's neck and straight into Joel's face. The canteen caught him squarely, and blood spurted in every direction. Joel howled as he tumbled off the back of his horse. Ethan jumped to the ground and grabbed the Winchester, kicking Finch's revolver out of reach at the same time. Joel writhed on his back, blood pumping between his fingers.

"Aw, hell," Ben said, dropping from his saddle.

"Stay put," Ethan ordered.

Ben stopped, but he looked half sick with regret. "I didn't mean it, Joel. Don't be mad."

"Would you have rather he shot me?" Ethan asked.

"He wouldn't have shot you," Ben flung back, nearly in tears. "He was just trying to buffalo you into letting me go with him."

"The hell he was," Ethan growled. "You saw the look in his eyes, same as I did."

Ben wagged his head in anguish. "I think I broke his nose."

"What I hope you did was knock some sense into his head."

"You son-of-a-bitch," Joel said, struggling to sit up.

"I didn't mean it," Ben pleaded. "Honest, I didn't."

"It doesn't matter what you meant, you dumb little shit," Joel moaned, tenderly prodding his nose. "Goddamn, it's all wiggly."

"Let's go back to town," Ethan said. "We can have Doc Carver look at it before we turn ourselves in to Jeff. That'll give us a chance to look in on Vic, too."

Ben's head swung around. "Hey . . . Vic?"

"Not too good," Ethan replied, reading his mind.

Some of the color seemed to drain out of Ben's face. "He ain't gonna die, is he?"

"Doc seems to think so. Me, I figure he's a Wilder. He'll stand a chance if he just hangs on."

Ben looked at Joel. "We gotta go back now. We can't leave Vic there to die alone."

Joel got to his feet, face a bloody mess, eyes already starting to blacken and swell. "You figure it'll make his dying easier if we're buried with him, huh?"

"Get on your horse," Ethan said, his patience finally wearing out. "We're going back, whether you like it or not."

Chapter Eighteen

The sun was still up but the shadows were stretched long before them. Approaching from the west, they came in sight of Cemetery Hill first, barely a knoll by Rocky Mountain standards, but the tallest point within an hour's ride of Sundance in any direction. The road, a trace cut across the prairie sod, wound around the north side of the hill, but Ethan guided his mount—he was astride the Appaloosa again, the Winchester booted under his right leg—off the twin wagon tracks.

"We'll keep that hill between us and town as long as we can," he said.

Ben, riding in the lead, glanced over his shoulder. "Pa's up there?"

Ethan nodded. It seemed a long time ago now that he'd tossed that handful of dirt into Jacob Wilder's grave, listened to the dry, bone-like rattle of clods hitting the top of the simple pine casket.

"Want to have a look?" he asked.

"Yeah," Ben said, then quickly turned away, lest someone see the moisture in his eyes.

Ethan glanced at Joel. "What about you? Want to pay your final respects?"

"Final's what it's going to be," Joel growled nasally. "But if it'll keep me out of Burke's jail a little longer, I'll do it."

"I want to say a prayer over his grave," Ben announced.

Joel snorted laughter, spraying the front of his already bloody shirt with another fine, pink mist. "You're too late, little Brother, if you think the Lord's going to change his mind about Pa. Likely he's already down in hell, threatening to whup ol' Lucifer's ass if he don't step out of the way."

Ben laughed at the image. "Maybe, but I still want to say a prayer. It couldn't hurt."

They reached the base of the slope and began to climb. On top, they paused to locate the freshly turned earth where Jacob had been laid to rest.

"Hey, that ain't a bad spot," Ben stated brightly. "We gonna get a headstone, Ethan?"

"Sure, we'll get one," Joel interjected. "Buy one big enough for the whole family, I say."

Biting his lip to keep from making a retort, Ethan reined his horse in front of the Barlow bay Joel was riding so that he could be at Ben's side when they reached Jacob's grave. They were plainsmen, and didn't dismount. A man didn't need to stand flat-footed on the ground to say his good byes, but Ben hung his head low, chin pressed lightly into the fabric of his calico shirt. Ethan glanced at Joel, who had stopped several yards away and was studiously avoiding looking at the raw earth where their pa lay.

"You going to say a prayer, Ben?"

"I'm already sayin' it, Ethan."

"What about you, Joel?"

"Do your own praying, and mind your own business."

Ethan shrugged, but he didn't feel like praying, either. Joel was right. Jacob Wilder had set off down his own trail years before, and nothing any of his sons said now was going to change his destination.

Stretching tiredly, Ethan backed the Appaloosa away from the grave. Following the direction of Joel's gaze, he found himself staring speculatively at the Merrick house, and, out of nowhere, an image came to him, that of watching Merrick's wife heading for the barn with a basket on her arm.

He'd figured then that she was going after eggs or some other grub they kept there, but, thinking back now, recalling how she'd come around the side of the house after he'd taken Lou's rifle away from him, he realized her basket had been empty on her return, carried lightly on her arm. She hadn't been going to the barn to fetch something. She'd gone there to leave something. Ethan frowned, recalling the red- and white-checked cloth at the bottom of the basket. The kind people used for picnic lunches.

Straightening, Ethan said: "Come on, Ben. I want to check something before we ride all the way in."

Joel looked up curiously. "You got something special in mind, big Brother?"

"It's probably nothing," Ethan replied vaguely, giving the Appaloosa its head.

They rode through the cemetery to the lane that led back into town, descending the hill to the narrow side street where the Merricks lived. If anyone noticed them, they didn't make a fuss about it. Ethan was hoping that, with the lowering sun at their backs, they wouldn't be easily recognized.

There was no fence to keep them out, and they rode around back and dismounted at the barn's closed front door, sagging into the dirt on rusting hinges. There was a smaller door built into the larger one, and Ethan handed his reins to Ben and drew the Remington. "If hell breaks loose in there, you boys skedaddle fast, understand?"

"Like hell," Joel said, giving Ben his reins, then digging Finch's revolver from the Appaloosa's saddlebags where Ethan had stowed it that morning. Ethan didn't protest, but waited silently until Joel joined him at the door.

"Soon as we get inside, I'll go left," Ethan mouthed.

Joel nodded. That was all the instruction he needed.

Ethan pulled gently on the weathered cotton rope, the latch inside grating softly as it was lifted out of its cradle. He gave the door a push, then ducked inside and stepped to his left, gaze sweeping the small interior. The light was poor—slanting rays dissecting the straw-carpeted floor, dust motes bobbing and swirling like drunken revelers. Ethan's heart felt like it was trying to climb into his throat as he eased deeper into the barn. There was no livestock—not even laying hens—but there was a rustling of straw toward the rear of the building, a rippling belch followed by a slurred curse.

"Who's there?" a raspy voice demanded.

Ethan and Joel exchanged glances. Ethan nodded to the right and Joel took off, keeping low. Ethan angled toward the pile of straw where the voice had originated.

"Woman?" The voice was demanding, impatient.

Ethan glided swiftly across the dirt floor. A pair of stockinged feet on top of twisted blankets came into view, a greasy tin plate and empty whiskey bottle sitting carelessly between the man's ankles. A carbine and holstered revolver leaned against a wooden support beside the bedroll, and Ethan quickened his pace.

From the far side of the barn, Joel said: "The woman isn't coming."

A heavy-gutted man with matted salt-and-pepper hair sat up, craning his neck toward the sound of Joel's voice. "Who is that?" he shouted.

Stepping close, Ethan kicked the man's gun belt into the shadows, tossed the carbine after it.

The man swung around, confused but not frightened, more drunk than sober.

"Who're . . . ?" He stopped, and his expression went slack.

When Ethan saw the blood-stained bandage on the man's mutilated hand, a sudden roaring filled his head, like the pounding of a locomotive. Voice grating, Ethan said: "Come on in, Joel. We've caught the bastard who shot Vic."

"Sum-bitch," the drunkard muttered. He tried to climb to his feet but Ethan shoved him back, sent him sprawling. He howled when his injured hand struck the hard ground, and Ethan took a threatening step forward.

"Shut up, bushwhacker, before I gag your mouth with my boot."

The man raised his injured hand to his chest. "Don't shoot, mister. I'm drunk."

"You figure that's any reason not to kill you?" Joel asked, coming up on the bushwhacker's other side.

"Lordy, but it is. A man hadn't ought to meet his Maker in the pitiful condition I'm in."

"He's an insightful sack of shit," Joel commented. "You sure this is the one, Eth?"

"I'd bet my summer's catch of pelts on it."

"Good enough for me," Joel said, flashing the gunman a sinister smile made all the more evil by the bruised, misshapened lump of his broken nose. "What's your name, lard ass?"

"Wilkie," the gunman replied cooperatively. "Bob Wilkie. My friends call me Bobby."

"Then I reckon we'll keep calling you Wilkie," Joel said.

"Aw, hell," Wilkie groaned, then belched loudly. Glancing at Ethan, he explained almost apologetically: "I get windy when I drink. You're them Wilder boys, ain't cha?"

"What happened to your hand?" Ethan asked.

"You ought to know. You was the one nearly took it off with that damn' bear gun of yours."

If Ethan needed any more proof of Wilkie's guilt, that was it. Holstering the Remington, he squatted in front of the bushwhacker. "I need some answers, and you're going to give them to me."

Wilkie's eyes widened warily. He was still drunk, but not so far gone that he didn't recognize the danger he was in. "I don't know nothin'," he replied defiantly.

"Who do you work for?"

"I said I didn't know nothin'."

"Yeah, I heard you the first time." Ethan pulled his Bowie from its sheath, remembering how swiftly a knife had broken down Nate Kestler's resolve last night.

Wilkie's gaze followed the hand-forged blade almost hypnotically as Ethan passed it back and forth in front of his nose. "What're you gonna do?"

"What do you want me to do? First, I mean. Do you want me to cut off your nose? Or maybe do some more carving on that crippled paw of yours? I don't think it's going to ever be much use to you, even if it does heal."

Wilkie licked nervously at his lips. "Christ, mister, it ain't me you want, it's Andrews. He's the one I work for."

"Nolan Andrews?"

"Uhn-huh."

"Where is he?"

Wilkie shrugged. "I ain't seen him since . . ." He gestured toward his injured hand.

The front door rattled, and Ethan surged to his feet. He sheathed the Bowie, drew his revolver, but it was only Ben, ducking inside. "Ethan?"

"Back here." He moved away from the straw pile. Ben stood at the door, peering through a crack between the planks. "What's wrong?"

"Saw some fellas out front, couple of 'em carryin' rifles."

Joel swore and cocked Finch's Colt, pointing it at Wilkie's head. "Let's kill this bastard and get the hell outta here."

"Hold on," Ethan said, watching Ben. "Where'd you see these men?"

"Across the street. There's a coal shed over there they were ducking behind."

Ethan remembered the shed, had taken advantage of it himself before approaching Merrick's house yesterday. "Check out back," he told Ben. "Joel, keep your finger off that trigger. We might need that pile of dung for a hostage if things get tight." He went to the front door, put his eye to the same crack Ben had used. The street in front of the Merrick house was empty. Maybe a little too empty. He studied the coal shed across the street but saw nothing out of the ordinary.

"Ethan, there's a couple back here, too!" Ben called.

"Keep your voice down," Joel scolded.

But it was too late. The men out front must have heard him, and knew they had been spotted. Even as Ethan watched, a tall cowboy stepped out from behind the coal shed and fired a shot at Merrick's barn. The bullet hit the wide front door several feet from Ethan, but the hard smack of lead into wood spooked their horses. The Appaloosa bolted first, then the sorrel and bay, heads thrown high and to the side to avoid the trailing reins. Ethan cursed as he watched the Appaloosa round the corner of the Merrick house, his Winchester and extra ammunition still on the saddle.

Joel cursed, too, and Ben looked like he was going to bawl. "They got us trapped, Eth!" Ben cried. "What're we gonna do?"

"You can shut your trap, for one thing," Joel spat. "Dammit, Ben, you're more help to our enemies than you are to us with that big mouth of yours."

"Both of you shut up," Ethan snapped, backing away from the wall. The barn was solidly built, but it was made of cottonwood planks, and even a moderately powerful cartridge would likely penetrate them. "I recognized that cowboy," he said. "His name's Clint. He's been acting like he's Kestler's right hand."

"That means Kestler's out there, too, or soon will be," Joel said.

Ethan came back to where Wilkie was still sitting on his bedroll. The gunman looked considerably more sober now than when Ethan and Joel first confronted him. "Start talking, Wilkie," Ethan said coldly.

"I work for Nolan Andrews. Met him some years back in Colorado when we was both workin' for the Mine Owners Union."

"Skull busters?"

Wilkie shrugged. "Some called us that."

"I don't care what they called him in Colorado," Joel said. "I want to know what he's doing here."

"Nolan sent for me. Said he'd been hired to run off some rustlers, and that he'd pay us a hundred dollars a month plus expenses. Said it wouldn't take long. That's why he was payin' so good."

"What rustlers?" Ethan asked.

"Them squatters down on the Marias. Hell, it was good money and the law didn't seem to care one way or t'other, long as we kept our noses clean in town."

"Who does Nolan Andrews work for?"

"He never said no names, but we met us a citified dude out on the range one time who was ridin' a Lazy-K horse. Nolan said he was from Bismarck."

Ethan scowled. "From Bismarck, riding one of Kestler's horses?"

"I'm tellin' you what I saw, Wilder. Nolan plays his cards close to his vest. Me 'n' the boys figure he's makin' a lot more money outta this job than we are, but, hell, we're doin' all right." He looked down at his bandaged hand. "Was, anyway."

"What are you doing in Merrick's barn?"

"Kestler's got some kinda tie to Merrick . . . something about his kid bein' sweet on the daughter."

"What about Vic? Who shot him?"

"One of the boys in the barn, I reckon. I was down by the crik, if you recollect properly. We didn't know he was your brother, though. We was . . . well, you was supposed to be the only one out there. Least that's the way we had it figured."

"So when Vic walked out the door that morning, you thought it was me?"

Wilkie nodded, then ducked his head.

Ben had been listening to the conversation from the rear of the barn. Now he came over. "What about Pa?"

When Wilkie didn't reply, Ethan kicked the bottom of his foot, hard. "What about it, Wilkie? Did you kill Jacob Wilder, too, then try to frame a boy for it?"

After a pause, the gunman said: "I reckon that about says it all. Was just the old man . . . your pa . . . when we got there. Nolan was determined to get him to sign a quit-claim deed to his land, but the stubborn old fool wouldn't do it."

"So you killed him?"

"Nolan did."

"Then framed Ben for the murder?"

"Ike caught sight of him sneaking in the back way, so we circled around and cornered him."

"Whose idea was it to frame him for Pa's murder?" Ethan asked doggedly.

"That was Nolan's idea, too." Wilkie looked up pleadingly. "Just about any plan that came up was his. The rest of us was just followin' orders."

"Even if it meant killing innocent men and women?"

Wilkie's voice dropped to a whisper. "We was hired to run off rustlers and illegal squatters, and that's what we did. We gave 'em all fair warning, though. They knew what'd happen if they didn't get."

Ben made a small noise in his throat. Ethan glanced at him. Ben had spotted the carbine Ethan had tossed aside earlier. He picked it up and brought it over, his face twisted in fresh anguish. Ethan looked at the gun and his expression turned to stone. It was a pump action carbine, .32 caliber.

Numbly Ethan put his hand in his pocket, fingers roaming the misshapened lump of lead Doc Carver had dug from Jacob Wilder's chest. His gaze bore into Wilkie. The gunman looked back in terror.

"W-What are you gonna do, Wilder?"

"I'm going to cut your worthless throat," Ethan replied calmly.

"Now you're talking," Joel growled.

Ethan stepped closer, pushing through a red mist of fury. Wilkie raised his hands defensively and Ethan grabbed the bad one, bending it back until fresh blood spurted from the wound, resoaking the already stained bandage. Wilkie cried out shrilly, and Ethan slid the Bowie from its sheath.

"Ethan?"

He stopped, turned. Ben stood a few feet away, looking puzzled. "Are you gonna kill him?"

"That's what you wanted, wasn't it?" Ethan asked harshly.

Ben shook his head. "Not like this."

"Do you want to shoot him?" Joel asked. He nodded at the carbine in Ben's hands. "Go ahead, do it."

Ben glanced at the .32, then tossed it away. He looked at Ethan, eyes brimming tears. "Ethan?" he whispered.

A tremor shook Ethan's lanky frame. Wilkie was on his back, eyes squeezed shut in fear and pain. With a ragged cry, Ethan threw the gunman's hand away, stepping back in revulsion.

"What the hell?" Joel asked, dumbfounded. He raised his revolver. "If you ain't gonna do it, big Brother, then . . ."

"No," Ethan nearly gasped. He was staring at Ben, at the sudden redemption shining in his brother's eyes. "We're not killers, Joel. Not like Andrews and his scum."

Joel's jaw seemed to come unhinged. "So we're just gonna let this snake slither away?"

"No, we're going to turn him over to the law."

"So some rich-ass attorney can set him free?"

"So that trash like this can get what's coming to them legally. If we don't, we're no better than they are."

"God dammit, Ethan, Pa is kickin' in his grave right now, and you know it. He's roaring to get let loose so he can do what's got to be done if his sons ain't got enough backbone to do it for him."

"Pa's dead, Joel, and . . . times have changed."

Joel's face hardened. He lifted his revolver, muzzle pointed at Wilkie's head. Ethan didn't speak. Neither did Ben, and Wilkie's eyes were still tightly closed. Finally Joel lowered the battered

Colt. "I hope to hell you know what you're doing," he told Ethan savagely.

Ethan nodded. He hoped so, too.

Then a shout came from the street. "Ethan! Ethan Wilder! Are you in there?"

"It's Burke," Joel said dully.

Ethan sheathed his Bowie.

"Ethan Wilder! If you're in there, answer me!"

"Get over in that corner," Ethan told Ben. "Keep an eye on the back lot and the west side of the barn. Joel, you do the same in the other corner. Watch the front and side. And both of you keep an eye on this one." He tipped his head toward Wilkie. "If he tries anything, kill him."

"This is your last chance, Ethan!" Jeff called.

Ethan walked to the front door, peered through the crack. Jeff stood in the middle of the street, his revolver still holstered, hat cocked at an awkward angle above his bandaged scalp. Rifle barrels seemed to bristle from the coal shed wall, at least the half that Ethan could see, and probably twice that many covering the barn from other directions.

"Come on out," Jeff said. "Let's talk."

"You come in," Ethan countered.

Jeff hesitated, then nodded and started across the street.

A man peeked out from behind the coal shed. "Don't be a fool, Sheriff. They'll take you hostage just like they done that other fellow."

"Stay where you are," Jeff ordered without looking around. His gaze was locked on the barn's small front door; he kept it there until Ethan told him to stop about twenty paces away. "Give it up, Ethan," Jeff urged. "If you try to hold us off, you'll only end up getting yourself and your brothers killed."

"Ben and Joel seem to think that's what'll happen if they do surrender."

"Look, I don't have it all sorted out yet, but I believe you about Ralph Finch. What happened at the jail last night won't happen again."

"I don't know if that's a promise you can keep, Jeff."

"So what's your answer? To shoot it out until no one's left standing?"

"We got one of Nolan Andrews's men in here. He's confessed to being a part of the bunch that shot Pa and Vic. Will you arrest him, too?"

"You damn' right I will, and, if he confesses and signs a statement to that effect, Ben will be set free immediately."

"What about Joel?"

Jeff shook his head. "I can't do that, Ethan. Unless other evidence turns up to clear him, Joel will have to stand trial for assaulting the Merrick girl."

"Have you talked to Suzie Merrick yet?"

"I talked to her on the day she signed her statement alleging it was Joel who beat her up."

"That's a lie!" Joel shouted from the barn's interior. "I never even saw her the other day. I tried to, but her old man pulled a gun on me, marched me to your office like I was a criminal."

"Jeff, when you talked to Suzie Merrick the other day, did you believe her?" Ethan asked.

Jeff hesitated a long time before answering. "It doesn't matter what I believe, Ethan. I just gather the facts to the best of my ability. It's up to a judge and jury to interpret them."

Ethan was silent as he considered the lawman's reply alongside their own rapidly diminishing options. Jeff had too many men for them to try to fight their way out, and any attempt to do so would only reaffirm the town's belief that the Wilders were little more than barbarians, incapable of settling down or adjusting to law and decency. The thought of such a legacy left Ethan feeling blue cold. This wasn't what he'd hoped to accomplish by bringing Joel and Ben back to Sundance. This was a mistake, a brief side trip gone terribly wrong. Options? They had only one, to put their trust in the law and turn themselves over to Jeff Burke.

"What's it going to be, Ethan?" Jeff asked.

Ethan peered through the gap between the planks. Jeff stood as before, but others had joined him. Ethan recognized Clint and a couple of other Lazy-K riders, but most of them were townsmen.

"Where's Charlie Kestler?" Ethan asked warily.

"He rode out this morning looking for you and your brothers. Most of his men went with him." He jerked a thumb over his shoulder. "All except Clint and Shorty and Oren."

"And Andrews?"

"I haven't seen him, but I figure he's around. He'll turn up."

"Do me a favor, Jeff?"

"What's that?"

"Talk to the Merrick girl again."

The sheriff nodded. "I'll do that, Ethan. I give you my word. Give yourselves up and I'll talk to her until I'm satisfied she's telling the truth."

Ethan nodded to himself, knowing it was the best deal they were going to get. He went over to the smaller door and pulled it open. "Come on in, Jeff. Let's talk about surrender."

Chapter Nineteen

Jeff made Ben and Joel give up their weapons, but let Ethan keep his, even though he did make him walk out front with his brothers and Wilkie, where he could keep an eye on all of them.

A murmur of hostility rose from the throats of the growing populace on the street. Most of them were armed, and Ethan couldn't help feeling a moment's resentment. Where had these fine, responsible townsfolk been last night when Kestler's mob of drunken cowboys had tried to break Joel and Ben out of the jail for a lynching? His gaze raked the restless throng, taking in the malice in their faces, the rigidity of their stance. He saw Sam Davidson up front with a shotgun, and, when their eyes met, Davidson called: "You want me to get a rope, Sheriff?"

"I want you to get out of the way, Sam."

"You ought to turn your back for a few minutes," said Murphy, the blacksmith. "We can take care of this ourselves."

"Hold on," Jeff said quietly to his prisoners. He moved out front. "Gentlemen, I want every one of you out of my sight, and I mean right now."

A roar of protest erupted from the crowd. "You can't order us off the street," Sam replied hotly.

"The hell I can't."

"What are you going to do, Jeff?" Tim Palmer called from the rear of the crowd. "Arrest all of us?"

"That's right, Palmer, every one of you. Maybe not today, but I'll make it my personal goal to arrest at least three of you at a time, give each of you your own cell, until the circuit judge shows up and fines you for obstruction of justice. Is there anyone out there who thinks I won't?"

There was an uneasy silence, then a whispering like the soughing of wind through the grass. Grudgingly the crowd parted.

Jeff glanced over his shoulder. "Let's go."

They marched through a narrow, jostling aisle of hostile humanity. Ethan heard Joel's name uttered more than once, and realized it wasn't him or Ben or even Bob Wilkie the crowd wanted. It was Joel, for what he'd been accused of doing to Suzie Merrick—one of their own.

Jeff led them down the middle of the road until they came to Hide Street, where he moved them onto the boardwalk. The crowd remained behind, and Ethan began to breathe easier. Then Ben glanced behind them and said: "Here they come."

Ethan turned. Expecting a mob of rushing citizens, he was taken aback by the empty street. Then he spotted a cloud of dust approaching from the south, and his heart sank. Even as he watched, the murky silhouettes of horsemen came into focus under it.

"Kestler," Joel said flatly.

"Keep moving," Jeff commanded.

They picked up their pace. With the jail in sight, Ethan figured they had plenty of time to get inside, bar the doors and shutters. He hadn't counted on the men Kestler had left behind, though—Clint and Shorty and the kid, Oren. The cowboys seemed to appear out of nowhere, spreading out in front of the jailhouse door, formidable as a locked gate.

Clint moved his hand to his revolver, although he didn't draw it. Almost reluctantly, the other two followed his lead.

"Sheriff, why don't you let me go?" Wilkie said nervously. "This is between Kestler and the Wilders. I don't want no part of it."

"That's unfortunate," Jeff replied, "because you're in it up to your nose right now, which is a damn' good time for you to start thinking about keeping your mouth shut."

Ethan glanced behind them. Kestler and his men were approaching swiftly, a tawny flood of horses and dust.

"Keep walking," Jeff said tersely.

They hurried now, Kestler coming in fast from the south, Clint and his boys unmoving before them. Jeff paused briefly at the end of the boardwalk, eyes flitting left and right. The jail sat across the street, on the northwest corner of Hide and Culver, barely thirty yards away. At Jeff's signal, they started across.

"Don't come no closer!" Clint called. "Let's just wait where we are until Mister Kestler gets here."

"Charlie Kestler's got nothing to do with this, Clint," Jeff replied evenly. "It will be you and your boys who are interfering with an officer of the law if you don't get out of my way."

Clint shook his head resolutely. "I'm sorry, Mister Burke, but Mister Kestler gave strict orders that, if the Wilders came back, I was to hold them until he could deal with them personally."

Behind them, Kestler's cowboys were entering town, a thunder of hoofs echoing between the buildings, just a couple of blocks away. Jeff's reaction caught everyone by surprise. He stalked the remaining distance to the jail's front steps, almost swarming up them to get at Clint. The cowboy took a startled step backward and, too late, raised his arms in self-defense. Jeff jabbed a hard right that tore through Clint's skimpy guard, and Clint's head rocked back as if it had come loose from its moorings. He stood there maybe two seconds, slack-jawed, knees partially buckled, then crumpled.

"Get him out of here!" Jeff barked to Shorty and Oren, and the two cowhands quickly grabbed Clint's arms and hauled him out of the way.

"Let's go," Ethan said tautly, but they'd barely reached the boardwalk before Kestler and his men were upon them.

For a long minute the junction was crammed with plunging, rearing mounts, swearing riders. Then Charlie Kestler kicked his lathered horse forward, and the pandemonium died.

"We'll take over from here, Jeff," Kestler said stonily.

"No, it's my job. I'll handle it."

A cold smile cracked the rancher's granite demeanor. "You can't stop me this time."

Jeff put his hand on his revolver, feet braced wide. "I'm getting a little tired of other people telling me my job, Charlie, so let's make this crystal clear. If you try to stop me, I'll kill you. I'll swear to that much, no matter what else happens."

"You'd kill me, risk your own life and reputation for a pack of rabid skunks like the Wilders? I don't believe it."

"I won't do it for the Wilders, Charlie. I'll do it for the law, and what that represents out here if this town is going to survive."

Ethan had been watching Kestler's men closely, wary of any sign of treachery, but the sheriff's words drew his eyes as irresistibly as food in front of a starving dog. Glancing at Jeff, he felt a moment's pride standing at his side. The citizens of Sundance—at least those who had predicted he would cut and run, rather than face Kestler's wrath—had been wrong. Jeff Burke had no intention of folding, but Ethan also understood that didn't mean he would be able to stop Kestler and his men if they rushed him.

A crowd that had tagged along at a distance from Merrick's barn was stopped on the boardwalk half a block down from the jail. In the silence following Jeff's pledge to stand up for law and order, it stirred, then parted to allow a knot of men to pass through.

Bob Wilkie whooped loudly. "Hey, Nolan, get me the hell outta here!"

Nolan Andrews didn't respond, didn't even appear to have heard. He came forward resolutely, heels loud on the wooden boardwalk, spurs jingling, his men a clutch in his shadow. Two of them, including the man with the torn cheek, carried shotguns. All of them were well-heeled with revolvers.

Behind them, the townspeople seemed to shrink back, and Ethan's hope for assistance withered. "We'd better get inside," he said quietly.

"Can't," Jeff replied out of the corner of his mouth. "The door hasn't been fully repaired yet. One of us would have to go around back and open it from the inside, and I don't think Kestler's going to allow that to happen."

Nolan Andrews and his men reached the end of the boardwalk and stepped down into the street. Several of Kestler's cowboys reined out of their way.

"What's holding things up, Kestler?" Andrews demanded, halting at the rancher's stirrup.

Ethan's gaze returned to the gunman. Andrews stared back, face still discolored from the beating Ethan had dealt him in the Bullshead. Knowing he'd given as good as he'd gotten made Ethan feel a little better about his own bumps and bruises.

"What the hell are you doing here?" Kestler said to Andrews, glancing around uncomfortably, as if loath to be seen in the gunman's company.

"I'm here to get this mess cleaned up so me and my boys can move on," Nolan replied. "I'm getting tired of the way things have been dragging on, waiting for"—he looked deliberately at Kestler—"certain people to decide how they want to finish the job."

Kestler's eyes burned in sudden rage as the killer's implication spread through his men.

Down the boardwalk to their right, Ethan heard Oren say: "What's he mean, Clint?"

Straightening in his saddle, Kestler snarled: "All right, enough of this foolishness. Turn your prisoners over, Jeff, or . . ." He paused, staring north along Hide Street.

Ethan glanced in that direction. Gerard Turcotte and Badger Dick Barlow were riding into town, rifles balanced across the saddles of their plodding mounts as if they were just aimlessly wandering in. But Ethan knew these men didn't wander anywhere without purpose, and he turned away to scan both streets in his view, Hide and Culver.

"Or I'll take them by force," Kestler finished at last, dragging his eyes back to the sheriff.

"You might," Jeff acknowledged. "But you won't live to see it through."

Ethan spotted Seth and Gabe at the entrance to Palmer's Livery, and wondered how long they'd been there. Scotty Dunham and François LaBarge stood in the door of the Bullshead, the muzzles of their rifles poking above the scalloped tops of the batwings like stubby cannons. Hank McKay reclined in a chair in front of Jenkins's Barbershop, a long-barreled fowler resting across his lap.

"Jeff," Ethan said.

"I see 'em," the sheriff replied quietly.

"Ethan," Joel said from where he stood facing Clint, Shorty, and Oren. Finch's revolver had somehow found its way back in his hand, while Ben kept an eye on Wilkie with Jacob's little .32 pump leveled on the gunman's belly. Joel nodded to the far side of the street, where Nate Kestler sat his palomino along the fringe of horsemen.

Eyes narrowing, Ethan moved to the edge of the boardwalk. "Nate! Nate Kestler!"

The younger man flinched when his name was called, eyes darting as if seeking a place to hide.

"Come on up here, Nate!" Ethan shouted. "Tell us what happened with Suzie Merrick."

"Ethan," Jeff cautioned.

Nate turned a desperate look toward his father, and Charlie said: "Leave the boy be, Wilder."

"That's going to be hard to do, Charlie, considering his involvement in all this."

Kestler's face turned even redder, his entire body seemingly swelling in anger; on the far side of the street, his son appeared to shrink down like a frightened rabbit under so much scrutiny.

Shifting his attention to Nate, Jeff called: "Why don't you come on up here, son? I'd like to ask you a few questions."

"Stay where you are, Nate!" the father roared. He moved his hand to his revolver. "Move away, Jeff, or I'll turn my men loose on this town and watch it burn to the ground."

Like he'd done in Lawrence, Kansas? Ethan wondered.

"Wait a minute," Clint said uncertainly. "Mister Kestler, nobody said Nate was involved in any of this."

"Nate isn't involved," Kestler shot back. "It's just a damn' ploy by the Wilders to divert attention from their own crimes. They're the guilty ones."

But a sliver of doubt had been planted in Clint's mind. Maybe it had been there all along. He shook his head, took a step back. "I ain't easy about this, Mister Kestler."

"You're not being paid to be easy," the rancher snapped.

"What happened down in the breaks with Janey Handleman?" Ethan asked loudly, as much for Kestler's cowboys as for the ranch owner or his son. "What happened that Tom Handleman had to keep an eye on his girl day and night for fear of Nate catching her alone and unguarded?"

"You son-of-a-bitch," Kestler growled, pawing for his revolver.

Nolan Andrews stepped forward with an eager grin, smoothly palming his nickeled Colt. "Let 'em howl, boys!" he shouted to his men.

"Aw, hell," Ethan breathed, then grabbed Ben by the arm and threw him to the boardwalk.

Gunfire erupted on every side, as if a single trigger had been pulled. An explosion of noise and powder smoke filled the street. Lead whined, slammed indiscriminately into wood, brick, flesh.

Ethan dropped to his stomach in front of Ben and shoved his revolver toward the street. He saw Nolan Andrews in the midst of the swirling dust and lunging mounts and swung his sights toward him, but, before he could pull the trigger, a Lazy-K cowboy's horse bucked wildly into his line of fire. By the time the horse had moved on, Andrews was gone. Another took his place, a tall gunfighter with a revolver in each hand, firing methodically toward the knot of defenders on the boardwalk. Ethan aimed, fired, and the tall gunfighter jerked hard. He spotted Ethan and swung both revolvers toward him, but Ethan fired twice more and the gunfighter collapsed.

The dust and smoke thickened, jelling into a monochromatic pall. Half a dozen cowboys lay wounded in the street; horses ran pell-mell, reins trailing; men fled, leaving their guns in the dust as they sought shelter. Only a handful remained, hardened and desperate. Charlie Kestler, Nolan Andrews, the man with the torn cheek, another Ethan didn't know, kneeling on the ground, bleeding from the mouth. A bullet narrowly missed Ethan's ear. He returned fire automatically, knew he'd missed even as he pulled the trigger.

In the street, Andrews was grabbing for the reins of a riderless horse. As he swung into the saddle, Ethan cried a protest and scrambled to his feet. He raised his revolver, cocked it, pulled the trigger; the hammer fell with a hollow snap, chambers empty. Nolan jerked his horse around, slammed spurs into its ribs. He headed north out of town, and Ethan flung his pistol away and raced toward the end of the boardwalk. As Nolan streaked past, Ethan launched himself from the boardwalk, caught a hitching rail under his left boot and threw himself over the street. Nolan saw him coming and tried to bring his nickled Colt around, but he was too slow. Ethan crashed into him like a falling boulder and the two men tumbled into the street, the horse squealing and kicking under them.

Ethan rolled free, stood. Still on hands and knees, Nolan kept grabbing for his revolver, but the fallen horse was nearly on top of it, flailing the air around it with iron-shod hoofs. When the horse finally regained its feet and bolted, Nolan scurried for the revolver. As he did, Ethan lunged forward, sending both of them spinning through the dust. Nolan wiggled free and crabbed after the revolver, but Ethan beat him to it, kicked it under the boardwalk.

Nolan surged to his feet, eyes blazing. Ethan stumbled backward, trying to put some distance between himself and the burly gunman long enough to catch his balance, but Nolan was on him in a flash, throwing a roundhouse swing that would have broken Ethan's jaw had it connected. Ethan managed to duck that one, but Nolan pressed forward, throwing punch after punch with machine-like efficiency. Ethan parried some, dodged others, took the rest in a mind-numbing blur of pain.

Nolan's fists were like sledge-hammers pounding at his chest and ribs, rocking his head one way, then the other. Nolan could have finished it quickly if he'd wanted to. Instead he paused to savor his victory, a skeleton's toothy grin splitting his face.

"You suckered me with a whiskey bottle the last time we fought, but it's gonna be different this time," the gunman hissed through his own mashed lips. "I'm gonna kill you with my bare hands, then I'm gonna spit in your face, the same way I spit in your old man's face the day I shot him."

Ethan swayed dizzily, blinking at the sweat and blood washing down over his left eye. Just a few feet away, Nolan seemed a hazy caricature of a human being, a slope-shouldered brute with fists the size of anvils, fire glowing hotly in his eyes.

He's gonna beat you raw, boy, a voice said from behind him. Ethan looked. He saw his pa sitting astride a chunky pinto at the mouth of the alley behind the jail, his old Hawken rifle sloped across the saddle in front of him. Ethan frowned at the horse.

"Dandy?" he mumbled, puzzled. Dandy had died fifteen years ago, after falling through the rotting ice of the Marias in spring.

You gotta get mean, boy, his pa insisted. *You gotta remember what I taught ya.*

"Yeah." Ethan turned, became aware of a bloody drool crawling down his chin, and wiped it away. He remembered what Ira had said after his last encounter with Nolan Andrews: *If it had been your daddy he'd tangled with, he'd probably be missing a few pieces of hide this morning.*

"That's true," Ethan said to himself. Jacob Wilder had been a bare-knuckle brawler, but he fought to win, and usually did. "And me?" Ethan mumbled. "I'm Jacob's boy."

Nolan's eyes had narrowed suspiciously. "You gone addled on me, Wilder? Who're you talkin' to?"

Ethan looked up, a lop-sided smile twisting his maimed features. "Come on and do it, gunman. Let's see how tough you really are." He stepped forward.

Nolan raised his hands in the precise stance of a trained pugilist—elbows in, knuckles forward, left foot forward for balance and thrust. He squinted from behind his fists.

Ethan threw a left that Nolan easily parried. Ethan edged to the side. Nolan pivoted to keep him centered. Ethan threw another left the gunman effortlessly blocked, then a right that he withdrew at the last instant. Nolan swatted empty air, and his eyes widened in surprise. Ethan stepped forward, slamming his foot at the gunman's knee with bone-crunching force. Nolan howled and fell, and Ethan swooped on him like an diving eagle. They grappled inside their own cloud of dust, punching, gouging, kicking—Queensbury Rules abandoned in favor of something more primitive, and more deadly.

With Nolan's thumb pressed into one eye, Ethan turned his head to sink his teeth into the web of flesh between the gunman's thumb and forefinger. Nolan cursed shrilly and tried to drive a knee into Ethan's groin, but Ethan twisted at the waist and the blow skidded harmlessly off the outside of his thigh.

They broke and Nolan staggered to his feet, but Ethan lunged before he was all the way up, wrapping his arms around Nolan's waist and driving him back and down. He began swinging, an unrelenting assault that slowly but steadily broke through the killer's defenses. Ethan pummeled Nolan's already misshapened face, felt the cartilage of his nose soften like mush under his fists, saw the tiny white blossoms of broken teeth in the dirt on either side of his head. Yet the gunman refused to surrender; his own fists flew with unmatched fury, hammering the air from Ethan's lungs, raining upward into his face, neck, and ribs.

Ethan pumped his fists ruthlessly, driven by a need to win no matter the cost, to set things right for Vic and his pa and for the hell they had all gone through. Nolan's punches became a distant thing, distantly felt. Like the thumping of a ball bounced off the side of a house. There was no longer any pain, no feeling at all save for the mindless pistoning of his arms. He drove them wildly downward until light turned into darkness and the darkness carried him away.

Chapter Twenty

It was like rising through a vat of black printer's ink, everything sluggish and warm until, near the top, something uncomfortable crawled into the caldron with him. He tried to push it away, but it followed. Sensations crowded after it, sounds and smells and an acidic aftertaste that seemed to burn the back of his throat. And pain, a giant's fist squeezing until there wasn't any part of him that didn't want to scream in agony.

It took a tremendous effort just to open his eyes, to force apart his gummy lids. Through the muck he saw starlight overhead, the faint vapor of his own shallow breathing. Gradually he became aware of a glow on the horizon, the crackle of flames, the soft touch of feminine fingers patiently stroking the back of his hand. Steeling himself for the journey, he rolled his head to the side. The light came from a small campfire. The fingers belonged to Rachel. She must have felt his slight movement because she immediately tensed up, lifting her bowed head as much in fright as relief.

"Mama, he is awake again."

Again?

A shadow eclipsed the fire—broad, rounded shoulders, the forward hunch of a sturdy body worn down by decades of labor. Corn Grower touched the top of Rachel's head in reassurance, then dropped to her knees beside him. The tips of her fingers glided over him like tiny antennas, feeling his forehead, neck, shoulders, measuring breath and pulse and temperature as thoroughly as Doc Carver ever had with his stethoscope and thermometer.

When she leaned back, she was smiling. "You sleep a long time, young warrior. We worry that you might not awake."

"Mama, don't say that," Rachel scolded, revealing her own anxieties.

"Is all right now, Daughter. Ethan has returned to the land of the People, and this time, I think he will stay. Yes, this time he will stay." She patted his arm with unexpected affection, then pushed to her feet. "You are thirsty, no? I bring water. Later there will be broth."

Corn Grower returned to her fire, and Rachel leaned close. "Do you hurt?"

He shook his head negatively.

She smiled and smoothed the hair back from his forehead. "Such lies," she said quietly. "You are very bruised, Ethan Wilder. Your chest looks like a sunset. Mama thinks maybe some ribs have been cracked. That is why it is so difficult for you to breathe, because of the bandages."

That and the pain, he thought to himself.

"Do you wish to know what happened after you were brought here?"

Ethan had to try twice to get the words out. "Did Nolan Andrews get away?"

Her face hardened. "No, the killer Andrews is in jail, along with . . ."

"No," he interrupted. "That's enough for now."

Rachel hesitated, then nodded. "The rest can wait."

He agreed silently. If the news were bad, he didn't want to hear it. Not yet. And if it were good, then Rachel was right. It would wait.

Corn Grower returned with water that he sucked down so ravenously she finally took the gourd canteen away from him. "You can have more later," she promised. "With broth."

"I ain't so hungry, but I could drink a lake dry," he told Rachel after her mother had left. "Where am I?"

"We are still camped north of town."

He lifted his eyes to the frosted sky. "How long have I been here?"

"Yesterday afternoon and tonight. It will be dawn soon."

"All right." His voice trailed off. "All . . . right." He wanted to say more, but sleep stole over him before he could gather the words.

* * * * *

Jeff Burke came in the afternoon, driving Doc Carver's buggy with the top down. Ethan was sitting on a cushion of grizzly bear robes under the shade of a canvas shelter fastened to the north side of Turcotte's wagon, back propped against the rear wheel. His body—every muscle, bone, joint, and tendon—throbbed.

"Feel like taking a drive?" Jeff asked, pulling up a few yards away.

"No," Rachel protested from the fire where she was helping her mother prepare the evening meal.

"Sure," Ethan lied.

"Ethan!"

"I'm fine," he told her, creaking to his feet like an old man. He hobbled over to where Jeff waited in the buggy, pretending not to notice Ethan's gnome-like waddle. Rachel walked with him, although keeping her hands at her sides so as to not draw attention to his weakened condition. He felt more confident when he was able to steady himself by holding onto the carriage's rim. Standing aside, he looked at Rachel. "Come with me."

She looked surprised by the request, but climbed into the buggy without hesitation. Ethan heaved himself carefully after her, then sank back gratefully into the leather upholstery, face shining with perspiration. With everyone seated, Jeff flicked the lines, and Doc's mare moved out briskly, making a tight circle back toward town.

"I reckon you know what happened?" Jeff said, more a statement than a question.

"No, I don't," Ethan confessed. "I haven't asked."

Jeff gave Rachel a quizzical glance, but didn't say anything. They drove down Hide Street at a trot. As they approached its intersection with Culver, the jail on the corner, Ethan frowned, staring at the mouth of the alley behind it. Noticing his reaction, Jeff said: "Something wrong?"

Ethan shook his head. "Naw. Just thought of my old man all of a sudden."

Jeff and Rachel looked back as they passed the alley, but Ethan had already turned his attention forward, the image of his pa sitting on Dandy already fading from his memory.

"Where are we heading?" he asked.

"Doc's."

Ethan's throat went dry, and he turned his face away lest they spy his fear. When they pulled up in front of the neatly painted house on the south end of town, he felt a lurch in his chest to see Ben rising from the hard wicker chair on the shaded front porch.

"Ethan!" Ben shouted, vaulting the railing rather than take a short step to the side to use the steps. He ran up to the buggy, all broad smiles and shining eyes, face freshly scrubbed, hair trimmed down to sod-buster length.

Nearly choking on his joy, Ethan said: "Who put you through the wringer?"

Ben tousled his own hair self-consciously. "Aw, Claudia Carver did this. Tried to skin me to the bone, but I wouldn't let her go no shorter'n this."

"Missus Carver," Ethan corrected.

"Uhn-huh, that's who I said."

Jeff guffawed and swung down from the carriage. "Take these, youngster," he said, handing Ben the lines.

Ethan was slower to step down, and Ben's expression sobered, watching his brother lumber away from the buggy.

"Dang, Eth, you walk like you're a hundred years old."

"I feel like I'm a hundred years old," Ethan acknowledged. He slipped his arm through Rachel's, and they made their way to the house together.

Doc met them at the door, eyeing the younger man's gait critically. "How bad is the pain?" he asked as Ethan passed.

"Tolerable."

"I can give you some laudanum."

Ethan paused only a second. "I wouldn't turn down a spoonful tonight to help me sleep."

Doc nodded. "I'll give you a bottle."

They went through the office to the small recovery room. Expecting the worst, Ethan came to an abrupt stop in the door. "Good Lord," he whispered.

"Not quite," said Joel. His nose was bandaged and his eyes were black, but he looked pretty good sitting in a chair beside the open window.

Vic smiled, seemingly as self-conscious at being caught abed as Ben had been about his haircut. "Hey, big Brother," he said, a new strength in his voice.

Ethan looked at Doc, who shrugged. "It was either attempt to operate on him myself or watch him die. I decided I didn't want to do the latter."

"You did it?"

"Two days ago, right after you left to fetch Joel and Ben from Elk Camp. I decided on making a small incision, then used tweezers to remove the bullet and bone fragments." He grinned with self-conscious pride. "For a blind old man with the tremors, it turned out all right."

"He's gonna live, though Doc says he's gotta stay in bed at least a week," Joel added.

For the first time, Ethan noticed the splint on Joel's leg, half hidden behind the bed. "What happened to you?"

Joel grimaced. "One of Nolan Andrews's gunnies fetched me a bullet to the leg. Burns like hell, but Doc says it didn't bust no bones, so I ought to be on my feet before long." He smirked, but cautiously, out of respect for his swollen nose. "Just not up to any heavy liftin' back home. I reckon you 'n' Ben'll have to tote my share of the work for a while."

"I expect we can handle that," Ethan said, the words jamming up in his throat so bad he had to look away.

"Let's let these two rest," Doc said, shepherding them out of the room.

There was a chair in front of Doc's desk. Ethan eased into it. Jeff sat down across the room and removed his hat, while Doc led Rachel into the parlor to find his wife.

"Rachel didn't tell you what happened?" Jeff asked when they were alone.

"I didn't want to hear about it last night, and couldn't seem to bring it up today. I expect I was afraid of what she'd tell me."

"Then you have some catching up to do." Jeff hesitated, debating where to start. Finally he said: "I talked to Suzie Merrick again. She pretty much confirmed what I'd begun to suspect."

"That it was Nate Kestler who beat her up?"

"No, that it was her pa. Her stepdad, I mean. Seems like Lou's been feeling his oats ever since Suzie started to fill out a dress. Nothing out of hand yet, but he was pushing her for it, and Suzie kept resisting. That's why he got so hot under the collar when he saw she was starting to favor Joel. Jealousy, I guess. I wouldn't know what kind of thoughts drives a man to do something like that. Anyway, Suzie's ma wouldn't press charges, but I sent Lou packing south to Fort Benton with the information that, if I ever saw him around Sundance again, I'd shoot him on sight." An uncomfortable look came across the sheriff's face. "I meant it, too."

"Joel's in the clear?"

"Completely."

"What about Andrews?"

Jeff smiled. "There's the good news in all this mess. Andrews and what's left of his crew are locked up, waiting for a U.S. marshal to escort them to Helena for trial. Charlie Kestler is with them."

Ethan's fingers tightened on the arms of his chair. "I knew that son-of-a-bitch was in on it."

"He was, for a fact. I told you I'd contacted the marshal in Bismarck. Well, Kirk kept digging for me, and it turns out Westminster isn't as big as they'd wanted folks to believe. It's actually owned by a trio of businessmen out of New York, one of whom happened to be Charlie Kestler's uncle, who also coincidentally happened to own stock in the Saint Paul, Minneapolis, and Manitoba Railroad."

"Then the railroad is going to build a spur to Sundance?"

"It's not a done deal yet, but talk is serious enough that the uncle wanted to get involved. Charlie was running squatters off the land to claim it for the Lazy-K, and, if the railroad did come through, he'd own the right of ways to some of the likeliest crossings on the Marias."

"Can you prove it?"

Jeff nodded happily. "I sure can. Turns out Gerard was wrong about Andrews and his men killing old Emile Rodale. They tried to, but that old cougar put the slip on them, then hightailed it out of there on foot. He turned up in Fort Benton a few days ago, lame and weak from walking all that way with a bullet in his shoulder, but clear-headed enough to tell the law what'd happened. It was Andrews who implicated Charlie Kestler, and he's got a telegraph and some banknotes drawn on both the Lazy-K and Westminster accounts to back him up. It ought to hold up in court just fine."

"Then it's over?" There was a note of doubt in Ethan's voice.

"Looks that way. You Wilders are free to go as soon as you feel like riding." After a pause, he added: "I'm sorry about your pa, Ethan, and I'm sorry about jailing your brothers. I want you to know I didn't have any choice but to lock them up until I could sort out what was going on."

"I've got no hard feelings on the matter, Jeff."

"Good, I appreciate that." He stood and put on his hat. "I've got to get back to the jail to relieve my new deputy. I reckon Ben or Rachel can drive you back to camp. When you're up to it, I'd like for you to stop by the office and fill out another Incident Report."

"I'll do that."

Jeff nodded and turned away. When Ethan heard the front door close behind the lawman, he leaned back in his chair. He felt suddenly wrung out, as if all his joints had come unhinged at the same instant. Hearing the soft pad of moccasins, he looked up to see Rachel standing in the parlor door, holding a tiny cup as fragile as a sparrow in both hands.

"Claudia thought you might like some tea," she said.

"You drink it."

"I've already had some." She came over and set the cup on the desk beside him. "Now what will you do?" She tried to ask it casually, but couldn't keep the wariness out of her words.

"What do you mean?"

"Will you go back to the Bar-Five?"

"I expect I will, soon as I can ride."

Rachel nodded and started to turn away. Ethan grabbed her hand, pulled her back. She stood at his side but refused to look at him.

"Of course," he said, "I wouldn't want to leave town until the minister got here. If I'm not mistaken, there's a circuit preacher due this Sunday from Fort Shaw."

Rachel looked at him uncertainly. "And you wish to confess your many sins?"

"No," he replied, struggling to his feet to take her into his arms. "I wish to marry the prettiest girl on the Marias. That is, if you'll have me."

She put her arms gently around his neck, and her eyes grew moist. "Yes, Ethan Wilder, I will have you. Forever."

THE END

About the Author

Michael Zimmer grew up on a small Colorado horse ranch, and began to break and train horses for spending money while still in high school. An American history enthusiast from a very early age, he has done extensive research on the Old West. His personal library contains over two thousand volumes covering that area west of the Mississippi from the late 1700s to the early decades of the twentieth century. In addition to perusing first-hand accounts from the period, Zimmer is also a firm believer in field interpretation. He's made it a point to master many of the skills used by our forefathers, and can start a campfire with flint and steel, gather, prepare, and survive on natural foods found in the wilderness, and has built and slept in shelters as diverse as bark lodges and snow caves. He owns and shoots a number of Old West firearms, and has done horseback treks using nineteenth century tack, gear, and guidelines. Zimmer lives in Utah with his wife, Vanessa, and two dogs. His website is www.michael-zimmer.com.

ce